LIONS · TRACKS

Andra

"How long is all your life, Kiroyo?" Andra asked. "Over three hundred years, isn't it? You should be dead. I should hate to be compelled to live so long in this dreary sunless city."

The old man looked up from his book. "It's the best we can offer you," he said. "The surface of the earth is no longer habitable."

"I know," Andra said. "I know, because two thousand years ago we destroyed it. We destroyed every living thing and condemned ourselves to creep like worms beneath the surface. My ancestors made me worse than a slug, never to see a tree or a flower growing under the sky, never to feel the wind, or the rain, to see the sun. Even the air we breathe is manufactured and the food we eat is synthetic. This is not living, Kiroyo. This is merely existing. I damn the man who dropped that bomb! He swung the earth from her orbit just to end one stupid war, and left us with a lump of useless rock!"

Louise Lawrence

Andra

LIONS · TRACKS

First published in Great Britain by
William Collins Sons & Co. Ltd 1971
First published in Lion Tracks 1991

Lions Tracks is an imprint of
the Children's Division, part of
HarperCollins Publishers Ltd,
77 Fulham Palace Road,
London W6 8JB

Set in Garamond
Printed and bound in Great Britain by
William Collins Sons & Co. Ltd, Glasgow

To my husband

LASCAUX

1

Lascaux made up his mind.

"Get Administration on the phone," he ordered the nurse.

The young woman's usually blank blue eyes showed surprise.

"Administration?" she dared to question.

"Yes," said Lascaux. "Renson. Garron. Anyone will do. I have decided to operate."

"Oh," the nurse said dubiously. "Very well, sir."

Lascaux returned to the theatre; to the heat, the glaring white light, the medical team hovering round the girl on the table. Their conversation halted.

"Respiration?" Lascaux inquired.

"Normal."

"Pulse?"

"Normal."

"Good. I am going to operate."

"A transplant?" asked one of the students.

It was Linli who had spoken, a young man with a surprisingly ugly face but the makings of a promising doctor. Lascaux supposed the question was in order. A brain transplant in a case like this was the most usual proceeding.

"No. A graft. Only a small portion of the brain is damaged."

"A graft? But surely . . ."

"A graft has never been successful before? You are right. A brain graft *has* never been successful before. But there is always a first time."

Lascaux frowned to himself as he pulled on his sterilised gloves. A graft would be tricky. Well, there was no harm in trying, nothing to lose. If it was unsuccessful the girl would be quietly expired unless Administration ordered her to be expired now. That would be a pity. He would like to try a graft.

He leant over his patient to pull back the closed eyelids and reveal the blue staring iris which would never see again unless the operation he planned was a success. This was one of those rare accidents, a skull fracture, a fragment of the occipital bone depressing the psycho-visular region of the brain. He couldn't remember when he had last had a child as a patient and it was her youth which had made him operate: remove the bone, relieve the pressure, only to find that the region which controlled her sight was damaged beyond repair. The girl would be blind and Lascaux knew the rules. The city would not support any person who was not physically faultless. She would not be allowed to live if she was blind.

His deft fingers probed the exposed part of the girl's brain. The damage was extensive. The whole region would have to be removed. It should be possible; tricky but possible. He would like to try. It was a challenge to his skill. He would like to be the first surgeon ever to perform a successful brain graft.

"Renson on the phone, sir," the nurse said.

Lascaux strode from the room and discarded his face mask. The clock on the wall said 2045 hours. It was already into the official time of darkness and the working day was over.

He picked up the phone.

"Renson? Lascaux here."

"How can I help, Lascaux?"

Renson sounded annoyed, but Lascaux was in no mood to consider Renson's temper. Had it been a matter of death it would have been routine. But it was a matter of life, and only Administration had the power to grant life. He wanted to operate and he needed their permission.

"Accident," Lascaux said. "A young girl with a fractured skull. Blind. Ought to be expired."

"Then expire her. You don't need my permission. That's routine."

"I want to operate."

"Eh?"

"Operate. Psycho-visular damage. I want to try a graft."

"A graft? But why?"

"A *brain* graft, Renson."

"I heard you. I asked why?"

"For the simple reason that a brain graft has never been done successfully before."

11

"And you think in this case it will be successful?"

"It could be," Lascaux said.

The red hands of the clock swept past seven seconds of silence.

Renson said:

"EDCO's report? Or is she employed?"

"I imagine she's in her final year at EDCO. I've sent for their report but I've not seen it yet."

"Why not transplant? C21/09/37 Vallonde is next on the list."

"Renson, do not be so unfeeling. This is a young girl. Only fifteen or sixteen years of age. I can't put a mature brain in her. It probably wouldn't fit, and anyway Vallonde was a man."

"Mmm. Confounded nuisance. Kiroyo could do with Vallonde's help right now. All right, Lascaux. Do what you want. You know the rules."

The surgeon put down the phone. Oh yes, he knew the rules. If his operation failed the girl would die. If he could give her back her sight she would be allowed to live: go back to EDCO, finish her education, be put to work and serve a useful forty-five years until she was sixty. At sixty, if she hadn't qualified to live on, she would be automatically expired. Whether she died now or in forty-five years' time made no difference to Lascaux except that it made him wonder if it was worth all his effort.

Was it worth it? Well, it would be interesting if

nothing else. If the girl lived he would have achieved something: a small amount of fame for himself. If he failed he had lost nothing, nothing but a few hours of his time. He put on a new face mask, pulled on a new pair of gloves and swung through the white double doors.

Lascaux nodded to Linli.

"Go and get it. Cranial capacity 146.978."

It took Linli an hour to fetch the brain from the organ bank. Even then EDCO's report hadn't arrived and Lascaux was operating without it.

The girl was breathing shallowly, in a natural coma and numb from their injections. Sweating profusely under the hot lights, Lascaux began to remove the damaged part of her brain. *Respiration weaker, pulse weaker.* She had been kept waiting too long all because he had to get Administration's permission. Damned red tape at a time like this. The girl's limbs twitched convulsively as the electronic scalpel dug deeper. The effect of the paralysing injection was wearing off.

"Another .5," Lascaux requested.

Someone filled the syringe and injected the drug into the girl's brain. Lascaux waited ten seconds and returned with the scalpel. Pulse faltering. He waited. Pulse steady. His deft fingers cut away the tissue. His knowledge of the functioning of the human brain was unrivalled, but even he could not afford to cut even the tiniest portion of the other regions which controlled her movements and her intelligence. Linli returned before he had

13

severed the spongy tissue and dropped it into a basin. The worst was over.

On a smaller table the other brain was waiting. He started to cut away the psycho-visular region ready for the actual graft. There was no bone here to hamper his movements. He was quicker.

"Read it to me," Lascaux instructed.

It was a nurse who told him about the being who had owned the brain. Her unwavering voice read monotonously from a punched card.

"Name: Richard Carson. Age: seventeen years."

It was an odd name. Lascaux had heard nothing like it. He knew no one with a double-barrelled name. Richard Carson had been about two years older than this girl.

"Sex: male."

Lascaux put down his scalpel and gave Linli a look which made the student cringe.

"This is a girl we have here, Linli. Kindly explain the stupid workings of your mind which made you bring a male brain."

Lascaux spoke calmly, but he had to fight to control the fury which welled up inside him and made him want to fling the useless organ right in the face of the stupid young man he had mistakenly thought might one day make a doctor.

"She had a small cranial capacity," Linli explained. "This was the only one they had which was small enough. I thought that as it was only a graft you were performing and not a transplant it

14

wouldn't matter whether the tissue came from a male or female. I'm sorry, Dr Lascaux. This is the only one there is."

"What is the cranial capacity of this boy's brain?"

The nurse read:

"Cranial capacity 147.039."

Approximately the same. It seemed that Lascaux had no choice.

"And the cause of death?"

"Freezing."

The tissue should be in excellent condition. Lascaux picked up his scalpel.

The nurse went on:

"Date of expiry: 1987."

"What?" roared Lascaux.

"1987, sir."

"I had to bring it. It's the only one suitable," Linli defended himself. "That's what took me so long. It's a bit old but there isn't another. I checked them all."

The only one suitable and it had to be prehistoric. "Bit old" was the understatement of the day. It was over two thousand years old. The boy must have lived when they first came underground or had they found his body in one of the cities on the surface and brought it in? What would it do to the girl? Lascaux struggled to remember his anatomy. Had men changed much over two thousand years? They had obtained a remarkable uniformity of appearance but he didn't think they

15

had changed. But what about their eyes? What had two thousand years of living under artificial light done to the construction of the eye and the brain tissue controlling it? It had weakened their power of sight but had it done anything to the brain tissue? Lascaux just didn't know and it was far too late to go into extensive research.

"IQ 140."

"Clever boy."

"Studying advanced botany and zoology. Keen naturalist. Accomplished guitarist and painter."

The data was obsolete. What was zoology? What was guitarist? He could ask Kiroyo but he didn't have time.

"Physical features: weight 159. Height 6/1. Eyes brown. Hair black. No deformities. No disease."

Nothing there to affect the girl. Her eyes were blue and her hair had been fair until they shaved her head. Everyone had fair hair and blue eyes except Kiroyo, and he was an oddity.

He held the psycho-visular region of the boy's brain in his hand. The actual graft was about to begin. Would her body reject the new tissue? Soon he would find out.

He moved her head slightly.

"Respiration shallow, pulse weaker."

Lascaux could hesitate no longer. The girl had been on the table for over three hours. Who was she? She was completely covered with a white drape except for the exposed portion of her smooth shiny skull and the grey oozing wound beneath the bone. He eased the new tissue inside.

"Pulse faltering."

"Heart machine, quickly."

They connected the coils and the great machine whirred, then hummed softly to massage the girl's heart and keep her alive. The bone grazed Lascaux's fingers through the glove. Someone wiped away the sweat from his forehead and Linli was breathing down his neck.

The loudspeaker blared.

"Dr Lascaux, the report you required from EDCO has arrived."

"Go and get it," Lascaux muttered.

A nurse swished away.

Graft. Ease the tissue inside a little more. Ease them together. They would knit naturally once firmly in place provided she did not move her head.

"Read it."

They took long enough sending it. Not that it mattered now. He had almost finished. He noticed the hesitation.

"Read it," he repeated.

"Citizen C22/33/5. Female. Age 15/4. IQ 65. Does not conform. It is requested that this person report to the duty office on her return. Her absence from EDCO was not authorised."

Lascaux was startled.

Damnation! If Administration knew they would be most annoyed. He had spent almost four hours saving the life of one of EDCO's failures. He wished he hadn't heard that report. He had been hoping to save a child who would one day provide a useful contribution to the community. This one was only average. She would end up in one of the factories, a menial worker among a million other menial workers. She was only average, incapable of thinking for herself, knowing only what EDCO put in her head. And yet she did not conform. She had left EDCO without permission. That in itself was an act of individuality. The report was wrong. If the girl was only average she had to conform.

The room was utterly silent.

"For someone so unimportant it hardly seems worth all your effort," Linli remarked.

"Unimportant? But she is not unimportant. To me she is *very* important. If she lives she will make medical history, and so will I."

In less than two hours Lascaux had finished the brain graft.

2

Linli said:

"The girl is conscious, sir."

Lascaux nodded absently. He did not even hear. He was busy with the information being pounded out by the computer. The computer told him the man's mind was antagonistic to their society. Lascaux had known the computer would tell him that. After forty years of living in Uralia the man was bound to be antagonistic, however much he denied it. He may have come here through fear of expiry, but another way of life was pounded into his heart and soul. He was too old to change, too old to completely accept life as it was in Sub-city One. Part of him would always be Uralian. Levinkov would be expired.

But the boy was more difficult. He, too, had come seeking political asylum. He, too, had been threatened with expiry. He was young. But was he young enough to become a citizen of this place and forget completely the country where he had been born? Lascaux didn't know and the computer was not sufficiently informed to give him a definite answer. Would he be accepted here and allowed to live freely? Would he be rehabilitated? Or would he be expired with his father?

"The girl is fully conscious, Dr Lascaux," Linli repeated. "You asked me to tell you."

Lascaux looked up in surprise at the sound of the student's voice. He had not heard him come in.

"What were you saying, Linli?"

"The girl with the brain graft is conscious. Do you wish to see her, or shall I take over?"

"I think," said Lascaux, "that I will handle this case myself. It interests me. I will go and see her in a few minutes. You, Linli, will go and talk to the boy who has come to us from Uralia. I would be interested to hear your opinion."

"Surely, if you rehabilitate him he could do no harm?"

"Mmm," murmured Lascaux. "Rehabilitation is not an attractive prospect. It destroys one's natural intelligence. The boy is a brilliant electrician. It would be a pity to take away his skill. Talk to him, Linli, before you request that he should be rehabilitated."

Lascaux picked up the phone and buzzed security.

"Dr Lascaux here. The man you sent me, the Uralian named Levinkov, is to be expired; probably with the three people tomorrow morning. Will you send the report to Shenlyn or shall I?"

"We can send it, Dr Lascaux. What about the boy?"

"I can't say yet. The computer reads negative. Besides, in this case Cromer ought to see him."

"Cromer is on relaxation leave, Dr Lascaux. He is not due back for another seven days. I will inform Shenlyn that you are waiting for Cromer to cross-examine the boy and there will be no results for at least another eight days. Thank you, Dr Lascaux."

Lascaux stood at the foot of her bed looking down at her. The chart in his hand told him the operation was perfect: no tissue rejection, no paralysis, no symptoms of mental disorder. For three weeks they had kept her unconscious, her mind incapable of any functioning but to heal. Yesterday they had given her the last injection and now she was conscious. There was nothing else to do now but wait; wait for the time when he could take away the bandages from her eyes and know if she could see. She moved her head slightly when he clipped the chart to the rail above her bed.

"Citizen C/22/33/5, can you hear me?"

"Yes," she said. "Are you Dr Lascaux? Linli told me you would probably be coming. What have you done to my head?"

Her voice immediately entranced Lascaux. She did not talk in the unexpressive monotone that most people did. Her words rose and fell and reminded him of some primitive music he had once heard as a boy.

"You should not be talking, my dear. You are recovering from a serious operation."

She sighed.

"You are like all adults. You cannot give a straight answer to a simple question. What have you done to my head?"

Lascaux stared down at her white-bandaged face and wondered what she looked like. He knew what she ought to look like: fair hair, blue eyes, a blank expression, but something told him this young lady was different. Just by the way she talked she became different. She did not conform. What right did she have, a mere girl child, to ask questions of him? On his collar was the silver badge of his rank. She should know that, even if she could not see it. She should know his position and know she could not question him. He heard himself answering:

"That part of your brain which controlled your sight was damaged. I have replaced it."

"You mean you have put a piece of someone else in my head?"

"That is correct."

"You should have asked me. I don't think I like it. I'm not me any more, I'm partially someone else. Whose was it?"

"That does not matter. Lie still. You must take things very quietly for several days yet."

She smiled at him briefly.

"If you don't tell me I shall ask Linli. He will tell me. I shall not let him carry out his routine examination until he does."

"Does not conform". How self-assured she was

in her defiance. She was insolent in her questioning and she was prepared to blackmail Linli.

"His name was Richard Carson. He was seventeen years old when he died."

The girl murmured:

"Richard Carson, that is a very strange name. It's not one name but two. Why did he have two names, Dr Lascaux?"

"I don't know and we don't need to know. Be still. I want to examine you."

"Linli examined me only ten minutes before you came in. I heard him writing it all down on the chart. Must I be examined again?"

"Yes," said Lascaux shortly. She will soon tell me how to do my work, he thought.

"Your hands are very cold," she protested.

He held her wrist. The beat of her pulse was quite regular. He could see her heartbeats moving the whiteness of her throat, relaxed and easy as she leant back against the pillows. He felt the sudden jump of her pulse as she raised her head.

"Who's there?"

Lascaux glanced round the room.

"Only me."

"No. There was someone else. I felt them. Who was it?"

"The nurse, I expect."

Lascaux was disturbed. No one had been inside the room besides himself and the girl on the bed.

"What is your name?" he asked her.

"Andra," she said.

* * *

23

Linli peered through his contact lenses at the fair-haired boy on the other side of the table. So he was Uralian. Linli felt a flicker of disappointment. He looked just like the young people in Sub-city One. He shuffled the papers in front of him. He felt awkward and he supposed the boy did too. It was the awkward awareness of strangers. "Talk to him," Lascaux had said, and Linli didn't know what to talk about. Just what help would his opinion be? Far better to rehabilitate him and be sure.

"You speak our language?" Linli asked.

"Of course," the boy replied.

"And you come from Uralia?"

"Yes."

"From which city?"

"Salynka."

Linli paused. He had established a few facts which were already down on the paper. He should try an original question.

"Is Salynka very different from Sub-city One?"

"In what way?"

Linli thought it should be he who asked the questions, not this boy.

"What I meant was," Linli said heavily, "does it *look* different? Are the buildings different?"

"I do not know. I have not seen Sub-city One, only a brief impression from inside a car. There seems to be more light and more colour here: the walls of this room, for example."

Linli glanced at the pale mauve walls. He hadn't noticed them before.

"What colour are they?"

"Mauve," Linli informed him. "Have you never seen mauve before?"

The boy shook his head.

"We have only white, grey and black," he said. "Everything is grey and the people wear black or white clothes. Our hair and our eyes are coloured, that is all. They say flowers grow in this city. Do they?"

"Flowers!" thought Linli. "We should not be talking about flowers." His interrogation was being sidetracked.

"Yes," Linli said shortly. "They grow in the gardens."

"Gardens?"

"Trees, flowers, grass, water fountains. Our people enjoy seeing them. Now tell me why you came here."

"I have already told Dr Lascaux."

"Then tell me also. Why did you come?"

"To seek political asylum."

That remark was obvious. Linli chewed his nails.

"Why do you need political asylum?"

"My father is a revolutionist. We had to come before they expired us."

"You say your father is a revolutionist. In what way?"

"He was one of the leaders of a plot to over-throw Grovinski. They planned to assassinate him, but they were found out, so my father fled here and brought me with him."

"You were involved with this revolutionary movement?"

"No, of course not."

"Then why did you come?"

"Because he is my father and as his son I, too, would have been expired."

"Would you really?" Linli asked in surprise. "That seems a little unfair."

"They take no chances," the boy said.

"You knew your father well, then?"

"No. He visited me on several occasions at the child centre and that was all. It was the fact that I am his son and I may have inherited some of his characteristics that made me a security risk."

"It all seems very unsatisfactory to me," Linli remarked, "but I will admit that I know very little about Uralian security. Have you met Cromer yet?"

"Cromer? No, I do not think so."

"He is head of our security department. No doubt he will be talking to you before long. How did you leave the Uralian city? Salynka, wasn't it? How did you leave Salynka?"

"We came by car, a fast one."

"You were not stopped? Why?"

"I am not sure. My father worked in the biggest

26

of the nuclear sub-stations along the arterial highway. It was usual for him to come and go. I assume he had some sort of official pass."

"And you wish to live with us in Sub-city One?"

"That is why we came."

"I hope your stay here will be a pleasant one," Linli muttered.

"What have they done with my father?" the boy asked.

"I know nothing about your father," Linli said.

Dr Lascaux opened the door. The Uralian boy recognised him. Linli did not matter now. He appealed to the older man.

"What have you done with my father?"

The tall man with pale eyes said:

"He is to be expired tomorrow morning."

The boy clenched his fists. His lips tightened.

"No!"

Dr Lascaux touched his shoulder.

Dr Lascaux is too soft, Linli thought.

"I am sorry," Dr Lascaux said. "Your father knew when he came that he would not be allowed to live. But he had hope for you. What is your name?"

"Syrd. Hope! That was stupid. We are both Uralian. He should have known. Will I be expired with him tomorrow morning?"

Lascaux shook his head.

"I do not think you will be expired. You will, perhaps, be rehabilitated. I can only hope you will not, but it is not my decision alone. Dr Massé and Cromer will be talking to you, and Shenlyn himself maybe. Our joint opinions will be fed to the computer. If it is found that you are genuinely willing to devote the rest of your life to the benefit of our city then we shall be happy to welcome you as one of us."

"They are no longer people," Syrd said calmly, "they are automatons. Grovinski is as inhuman as a computer."

Lascaux nodded.

"I hope you mean what you say. And now I think you have had enough questions for today. You are free to go where you like within the confines of the mental therapy unit. You will be required to answer more questions in the days to come, but between these interrogations you may do as you please. If there is anything you require, please ask one of the staff."

"Thank you, Dr Lascaux," the boy murmured.

"Oh, and Syrd?"

"Yes?"

"At the end of this corridor, in a room with pale green walls, there is a girl. Her eyes are bandaged and she is recovering from an operation. She will be unable to see for many weeks and I do not think she will be happy being blind. She may brood. In a few days, when she is stronger, she will be glad of someone to talk to now and then. Someone to provide some interest apart from her own thoughts. Talk to her, Syrd, but do not stay too long at one time."

"I will be pleased to do what you ask, Dr Lascaux. What is her name?"

"Andra," said Lascaux.

3

Dr Massé fell into step beside the other surgeon.

"I hear I have missed some excitement. A brain graft! You have all the luck, Lascaux. It is something I have always wanted to try. It went well?"

"Very well," Lascaux said. "I am on my way to see her now. Why don't you come along?"

"And where else did you think I was going?" Massé inquired.

The blue corridor turned to green.

"We had one little difficulty," Lascaux said. "Her cranial capacity was small. We had to use the brain of a boy who expired in 1987."

Massé raised an eyebrow.

"Then you have had the devil's luck to get away with it. *Have* you got away with it, Lascaux?"

"I think so. The graft itself has taken well. Of course we won't know the ultimate result until the bandages come off, but I have hopes, Massé, very high hopes. The girl is responding to treatment in every way. She has developed a remarkable sense of perception. She will know you are with me even if you don't speak."

Lascaux opened the door.

"Hello, Dr Lascaux," Andra said.

"Hello, Andra." He sat beside her on the bed. "How are you feeling today?"

"I am bored. Who is with you? It ought to be Linli but he hasn't asked me how I am."

Massé smiled. Lascaux had been right. She had perceived he was there even though she could not see him.

"I am Dr Massé, my dear. One of Dr Lascaux's fellow-surgeons. I see you are making remarkable progress but you must remember to refer to our absent friend as *Doctor* Linli."

She laughed.

"Linli is too young to be a real doctor. Dr Lascaux, how old are *you*?"

Massé's face turned red. No one should dare to question Lascaux so personally. He waited for the angry reply.

"One hundred and nineteen years older than you."

"So you've only been rejuvenated twice. I thought you were older. You are not even half as old as Kiroyo."

Massé shook his head. Lascaux was forgetting his position. This child should be reprimanded. She looked a very young child. Surely she had not left EDCO? And if she had not left EDCO how had an accident like this happened? EDCO's safety regulations were infallible, yet this child had had a fractured skull.

"How did your accident happen, my dear?" Massé asked curiously.

She bit her lip.

"I shall not tell you. Dr Lascaux will be angry with me."

"You will tell Dr Massé," Lascaux instructed. "I know you left EDCO without permission, but I would like to know why."

She pouted.

"It was Es," Andra said.

"Es? Who is Es?"

"She is my personal tutor at EDCO but she takes us all for geometrical design. She was designing on the wall board. They said she was boring."

"Who did?"

"The two boys who sit behind me. They are very clever. Their IQs are over 135. They said Es was boring. They made a bet I would not dare to leave the room."

"Who did?"

"The two boys. So I went. I walked right behind Es and she never noticed. I was standing in the doorway and everyone was laughing. Even then Es never noticed. Then I went into the corridor and out into the street. There was no one on duty at the main door. No one saw me."

"You should be severely punished," Massé said sternly. "Young people are not permitted to leave EDCO without an official pass."

"Hush!" Lascaux instructed the other surgeon. "Go on, Andra!"

"I was going to go to the gardens," Andra said, "but I saw the lorry standing in the street so I climbed on. It was something we had always wanted to do . . . ride on the lorries. We used to watch them from the relaxation room, those big lorries going by. They used to make the walls tremble. It was going to the rocket site. I rode all the way through the city and we went up in the lift. My stomach felt funny, but I liked it. Once we passed a security man and I hid behind a pile of plastic grass. No one knew I was there."

"But why did you want to go to the rocket site?" Lascaux asked her.

"I didn't," Andra said. "I was going to the gardens. I told you that. I didn't know the lorry was going to the rocket site."

"Did none of the men question your being there?" Massé snapped. He had no time for these childish escapades.

"No. I was talking to them. They thought it was funny. The driver wouldn't believe he'd brought me all that way. They were laughing at him. There was a man called Buven. He was very fat and when he laughed his tummy wobbled. He gave me a sweet and it fell on the floor. Then I don't remember any more."

"A metal bar fell on your head from the scaffolding," Lascaux said. "You were very foolish, Andra. I am sure you will not leave EDCO again without permission."

"EDCO," Andra said, "wants blowing up. I never realised until now what a deadly boring place it is. I shall leave whenever I have the opportunity, with or without permission."

Massé spluttered.

"You could have been killed," Lascaux said softly.

She shrugged her slight shoulders.

"And if I am blind I shall be expired anyway. Dr Lascaux, where is Richard Carson?"

Lascaux had realised that Andra had developed a keen power of perception, but she should not be able to sense the presence of someone who was dead. It was as though she expected him to be in the room. Richard Carson had been dead for two thousand years.

"Richard Carson?" Massé inquired. "What is the girl talking about?"

"It was his brain we used for the graft, Massé," Lascaux explained. "Andra, this boy no longer exists."

Lascaux paused. Was he dead? A small piece of his brain had been resurrected inside Andra's head.

"He's dead," Lascaux said firmly. "He only helped to save your life. It will not help to think about it. It's over."

She seemed angry.

"But it's not over. It's only just begun. He's not dead. He's here. I know he is. He's trying to tell me something. If I empty my head of all thought I almost know, but it slips away and I can't reach it, just a note of music or a flash of colour, never a complete picture. Dr Lascaux, you made him, now tell me what he is saying. Tell me why I want to go up and see the sun. At EDCO I never even thought about the sun. I never thought about anything. Tell me why these colours flicker in my mind. Tell me where he is and what he is trying to say."

Lascaux stood up. Massé, he knew, would be itching to discuss this case. He had performed a graft of the psycho-visular region of her brain. He had not touched the centre of her intelligence or her memory. There ought to be no personality change. There *could* be no personality change. Andra would need a stringent course of mental therapy.

"There is no one in this room besides Massé, you and me," Lascaux said coldly.

"Isn't there?" Andra asked. "Or is it you who are blind and not me?"

Massé had heard enough. What was this city coming to? What was EDCO coming to to produce a person like this girl? What was Lascaux thinking of to allow her to talk to him in such tones of insubordination? He strode down the corridor. He would have to have a serious talk with Lascaux. The graft may have been technically successful, but the girl needed to be rehabilitated, and the sooner the better.

Lascaux stayed a moment longer. Andra's IQ was higher than 65. EDCO must have made a mistake. And Richard Carson was dead.

"Dr Lascaux, are you angry with me?" Andra asked.

35

"No, Andra," Lascaux replied. "I am not angry with you. I am perplexed."

Syrd stood in the open doorway and she turned her head. He had come several times but he had not spoken to her. Her arms were bare and he had never seen a girl with bare arms. She made him feel awkward and he didn't know what to say.

"Why don't you say something?" the girl said. "I know you're there. Who are you?"

"Syrd."

"What a funny name. Your voice sounds funny too. Are you another doctor?"

Syrd approached the bed. She was only a girl.

"I have come from Uralia with my father. We came along the arterial highway five days ago. Are you Andra?"

"Yes. How did you know?"

"Dr Lascaux told us about you. You are making medical history. He took a piece of your head away and put another piece in. If you had been in Uralia they would not have bothered. Phut! You would have been expired."

Syrd walked right up to the bed. He should have talked to her before. There was nothing alarming about her except her facelessness, so if he did feel awkward she would not be able to see.

"Does it hurt?" he asked.

"Does what hurt?"

"Your head. I have never felt pain, not real

pain. Only once when I had a new pair of boots and they pinched my feet. Is pain hard to bear?"

"My head doesn't hurt. It doesn't hurt at all. My eyes ache from being shut for so long, but that is only a small inconvenience. Dr Massé and Linli sniff when I complain. They do not understand how completely boring it is lying here and all I can see is black. Should you be here? I mean, shouldn't you be locked in a security room?"

"Why should I be?"

"Aren't you dangerous?"

Syrd flushed.

"Dr Lascaux asked me to come in and talk to you."

"Did he? That was very thoughtful of him. Why haven't they expired you?"

"They expired my father but they won't be expiring *me*. I may be rehabilitated."

"Oh," Andra murmured. "That's not very nice. You would be better off expired, but I suppose you will be happy, you won't know anything once it's over. It's just thinking about it that makes it so horrible."

"What do they do?"

"I've no idea. No one at EDCO has. It's a threat they use: 'conform or be rehabilitated'. I keep meaning to ask Dr Lascaux. You should have quietly infiltrated, then they mightn't have noticed you. Or would they? What do you look like? Like us or different?"

The girl's easy way of talking confused Syrd,

but the tone of her voice fascinated him. He had never heard anyone talk as she did. It was almost like singing. No, not singing, like music, like the music of his vinet, sometimes high, sometimes low. But it was softer and more expressive than the vinet.

"What did you say your name was?" she asked him.

"Syrd."

"Syrd, tell me what you look like. I promise I won't laugh."

"My hair is red. My skin is green. I have three eyes, four ears, my tongue is forked and I have thirty-five fingers on my right hand."

She did laugh.

"Oh boy! I can't wait to see you. I hope you are still around when they take the bandages off my eyes. Why did you leave Uralia?"

"If I hadn't I would have been expired in a few days. Phut! I could not stay. What work do you do?"

"None. I am still being educated. I hate EDCO. There's no room to breathe. I shall be glad when I leave. At least when I go to work I shall have a bedroom of my own. But then I shall probably hate work too. What do you do?"

"Electronics. Computer electronics mostly."

"How utterly uninteresting."

"I play the vinet and sing."

"You what?"

"I play the vinet and sing."

"Do you? Do you really? Will you play and sing for me? I am so bored lying here I could scream. Only Dr Lascaux ever stays and talks to me. Linli can't be bothered. He says I talk through my hat and he won't listen. Come again and talk to me, Syrd. Play the vinet for me."

"I have no vinet. I left it behind in Salynka."

"I shall tell Dr Lascaux to get you one. Then you can play for me. Maybe you could teach me too. Would you teach me, Syrd?"

"If you wish. Do you like music?"

"No. But then I have never really listened to it. I don't understand it, but it will occupy my hands. Without my eyes they do not know what to do."

Syrd stared through the open door to the corridor beyond, a blur of white light and green walls. A feeling of unreality swept over him. The colours were strange to his eyes and hurt to see. The comparative freedom of the place unnerved him. He walked through the corridors as though walking through a dream. In Salynka he had always known what would happen next, each minute was part of a rigid routine. Here he knew nothing, he expected nothing.

The silence was long. In another room along the corridor he could hear the whirring of the computer, the sound of people talking, slow footsteps, hurrying feet, the soft swish of wheels and muffled metallic noises. Syrd gripped the back of the chair.

"Is it strange and horrible here?" Andra asked.

"Do you want to go home? I don't think I'd like to land in a foreign place where I didn't know anyone. You don't know how we live or how we conduct our day. Do you wish you'd never come?"

Syrd stared at her, the girl without eyes. How did she know how he felt? How did she know?

"How did you know?" Syrd whispered.

"I just knew."

"If Dr Lascaux knows too it will be the end."

"Dr Lascaux isn't an ogre. If he knows he will understand. I'm not very keen on Sub-city One either. It's too cramped, too restricted. You can't *do* anything."

"It's just the strangeness," Syrd said. "It's so vastly different from what I've been used to. The colours. I've never seen colours like them. Dr Linli took me to the gardens today. There were flowers, and trees. It was all green and coloured."

"Tell me about them," Andra instructed. "Tell me everything you saw. It's months since I went to the gardens."

Syrd told her about the gardens, about the colours of the flowers he had never seen before. About the great gleaming buildings of Sub-city One and the drab greyness of the city he had left behind. But always he came back to the gardens. To him they were nothing short of paradise. And the colours Syrd described whirled in Andra's mind forming pictures, pictures so strange she could put no names to them. Flowers and plants weird beyond all her imagination were clearly defined for a brief instant of time. There was a wildness and freeness inside her and she wanted to tear the bandages from her eyes and see the sun. She heard music, a strange rhythm beating like her heart and slipping away again. This was what he had been trying to say, not in words but in pictures. If she put out her hand, could she touch him? Or was he only inside her head, part of herself and not real to anyone else?

Her face was white and sad because the things she had seen did not exist. They were beautiful and only a dream. It made her want to cry.

"Are you all right?" Syrd asked her.

A tear seeped from the bandage round her eyes.

Dr Lascaux came in and sat on the bed.

"Why are you crying, Andra?"

And she could not tell him because she didn't know the words.

4

"Not the third finger, the second finger. Try again."

Her delicate fingers moved over the strings she could not see, depressed one and strummed a metallic note. Syrd covered his ears with his hands. That was not music, that wail of protest. It was a cry of pain from his poor vinet. Andra had no idea.

Syrd sighed and said patiently:

"That was the wrong string. The second string, not the third. Try again."

The note of music was harshly loud.

"You will ruin it. There is no need to hold the string right against the base. As you bring your fingers across, ease the pressure a little. Try it again. Play the five notes one after the other."

She obeyed him.

"That was horrible," Syrd said.

Andra muttered something to herself and tried again. Five quick notes flowing together.

"Again!" Syrd commanded.

She did it again.

"I do believe you're getting it. Now, as I call the notes, you play them. Three, four, two, one, three, four, two, three, four, five. Five! Five, girl, not four!"

"Don't shout at me. Say it again."

"Three, four, two, one, three, four, two, three, four, five. Five! I give up! I really do give up. Three whole days and you can't even play a sequence."

"Does it matter which one comes at the end? That was almost a tune. I thought it was quite good."

"It wasn't supposed to be *almost* a tune. It was supposed to be *quite* a tune. You just haven't got the feel of the thing."

"Bloody vinet!" Andra said. "Here, you have it. I'm sick of the plunky twangy sounds it makes. It's awful. Why does it sound so different when you play it?"

"Because I know how to and you don't."

"Oh, go back to Uralia! What are you doing, anyway?"

"I am making a design. Dr Lascaux gave me a box of colours."

"Syrd, sing for me," Andra asked. "Play that tune you played yesterday. Have you made up the words yet?"

"I was writing all the evening. I think it is the best song I have ever made."

Andra bit her nail.

"I still don't see how you make it play. But sing, Syrd. Show off, if you must."

Syrd grinned, closed the colour box and reached for the vinet. How different this city had become since he met Andra. Through her he had come to know it. How violently she magnified its faults.

She spoke in a way he would not dare. He wondered what she looked like. Was she just the same as the other girls he had seen that day in the gardens: short fair hair, blue eyes? But no, she couldn't be. She was Andra, and she was different.

His deft fingers found the strings and the music came. It was the best song he had made and he sang it for Andra.

"Omyara: you come whirling patterns in my
    mind.
You call through my dreams
With echoes that run
Like my footsteps that come far behind you
As through the curving passages of time
I chase to find you: Omyara.
Omyara, I run through the maze of colours
And the intermingling shapes of weird design
For you . . .
Something even music can't define,
Some vague translucent shadow in my mind.
I run through metal roads
And through the curving passages of time.
Omyara: take me in;
Let me sink into the darkness that is you.
I have run, I have run, for so long I have run
Through the curving passages of time.
And when I found you, Omyara, you were
    gone.
Omyara, Omyara, you were gone."

Dr Lascaux said:

"That was very good, Syrd. You show great talent. You will be popular here with your music."

"I shall tell Daëmon about you," Andra said. "He will let you sing at the youth centre."

Syrd stood up. The man beside Dr Lascaux wore a gold badge on his collar. His rank was even higher than the doctor's. His rank demanded that he should stand. He was a tall man and his eyes were a bitter cold blue. The expression on his face was one of scorn and his uniform was purple. The silence in the room was respectful except for Andra. She never had any respect and she could not see who was there.

"If that is Linli with you, Dr Lascaux, tell him to go away. I refuse to speak to him ever again. He promised he would come and tell me about the drama before I went to sleep last night and he didn't come. Linli, you are as deceitful as a tube of iron filings mixed with nitric acid. I hope your dinner makes you vomit."

"Andra," said Lascaux coldly, "be quiet, please. This is not Dr Linli. Syrd, this is Cromer, head of our security department. He has returned this morning from relaxation leave. You will go with him now and answer any questions he may ask you. Cromer, the computer room is vacant if you wish to use it."

Cromer inclined his head.

"You will come now," he snapped to Syrd. "Lascaux, that child on the bed is disrespectful.

Kindly inform her to improve her manner of speech if ever we should have the misfortune to meet again. Is she your brain graft?"

"She is," Lascaux confirmed.

"And her personal tutor at EDCO? Who might that be?"

"Es," said Andra gleefully.

"Mmm. I will speak to Es before this girl returns there. This boy will not be returning until 2000 hours. After my interrogation Shenlyn wishes to speak with him. Good day, Dr Lascaux. My regards to Massé."

Andra listened to the thud of their feet receding along the corridor. Dr Lascaux put the vinet in her restless hands. Why did Cromer always irritate him? It was as much as he could do to be civil to the man. Cromer was as unfeeling as the stone fountain in the gardens spurting its icy water.

"Poor Syrd," Andra murmured. "He will not be spending a pleasant day. I think Cromer is a nasty man."

"And you, Andra, are a nasty young lady. You have put Es in trouble with security."

A wide grin spread across Andra's face.

"Es should not be so boring. I will tell Daëmon about Syrd's song. I'll write to him. It was good, wasn't it?"

"Very good, but the words I found a little difficult to understand."

"I know what he means," Andra said softly. "I know exactly what he means. You can chase after something all your life, and when you catch up with it it isn't there. It's gone like a dream. I've seen it. But Omyara is a lovely name. It will catch on. You'll see."

She strummed an idle note.

"What is Shenlyn like, Dr Lascaux? Is he another nasty man like Cromer?"

Lascaux frowned to himself. Why didn't Andra show more respect?

"Shenlyn is Shenlyn," Lascaux said. "He is himself and not like anyone else, except maybe you, Andra."

5

Andra's fingers plucked at the resilient material which covered her. She could hear Dr Lascaux moving about in the room, but she could not see him. She could not see anything except the horrible black bandages which covered her eyes, and the pictures she made up in her mind. She was restless and sour-tempered.

"Where is Syrd? He hasn't been to see me for two days. Have you changed your mind and expired him? What are you doing? I refuse to let you examine me again."

Lascaux sat down beside her and took her hand. How infuriating it must be for her to stay in bed for so long. How boring time must be to her.

"Syrd is undergoing an intensive course of mental therapy. I told you yesterday. Shenlyn has permitted him to leave the centre in another nine days. You know he cannot come and visit you."

She pulled her hand away.

"I'm not a baby; don't pat my hand like that. Dr Lascaux, how much longer? I want to scream."

Lascaux stared at her slender hands, the fingers so delicately formed, so long with tapering nails. She had mastered the vinet. She could play it almost as well as the Uralian boy who had taught her, but she said it had no feeling. It was just a metal music-maker without a soul. It was too inanimate to make real music. It lay discarded by her bed. Andra could not catch the wind with her vinet.

Lascaux had learnt much about Andra from the unfortunate Es who had been sent in for a course of therapy. He found that she was fluent in the Uralian language and also capable in design. In all other subjects she was completely uninterested. She was destined to be put to work at commercial design. Es insisted that Andra was only average in her intelligence, but Lascaux suspected she could be extremely clever if she wished to be. He wondered how she would react to the dull routine of work.

Andra pounded his arm with her fist. The thoughts were driven from his head by the force of her blows.

"Take it off. Take it off. If you don't I shall scream the place down. If you don't I shall tear it off. I can't stand it any more."

Lascaux gripped her wrists.

"Be still, Andra."

He shook her gently.

"Be still, will you? That's better. The bandages are troubling you?"

"They always trouble me. I've been sitting here on my bottom for over three weeks, and a month before that which I didn't know about. I'm tired, Dr Lascaux. I'm tired of chasing after things in my mind which I don't understand, and never will until I can see again."

Lascaux pressed the buzzer above her head.

"*Now* what are you doing? Dr Lascaux, I'm sorry. What are you doing?"

"You want the bandages off, my dear, you shall have them off. They could have come off two days ago but you seemed contented enough then so I did not worry you. The longer your eyes are covered the stronger they will become." He said to the nurse: "Ask Dr Linli to come, also Dr Massé if he is not operating. I shall need scissors and some more dressings."

Andra was leaning back against the pillows, smiling at him.

"Do you really mean it? Are you going to take them off now?"

"Yes," Lascaux said simply.

Already he could feel the tension building up inside him.

How foolish! He had been operating for many years. He had had failures before. Why should he worry if this one was a failure? Was it because this operation was unique or was it because of Andra? If the operation had failed and she was blind he would have to expire her. Her IQ was not just normal, it was above average, which gave her a personality of her own. It made her different in such a way that she could never conform. She could be invaluable to the community if they found the right field. But if she were blind she would be dead. Lascaux was annoyed with himself. He had expired hundreds of thousands of people. Why should he mind just one more? He knew the answer. He would mind because she was Andra, and he would refuse to do it.

"Are you afraid?" he asked her.

"A little," she replied.

"So am I," Lascaux said.

Lascaux dimmed the light to a pale blue gloom.

It was Linli who unwound the bandages. Slowly, layer upon layer was peeled away. He was reluctant. What if Lascaux had failed? Why was it he who had to uncover her eyes to know if she could see or if she was blind, if she could go on living or if she would have to die? Her face was marked with lines and there was a mole on her cheek. Linli saw it as a blemish. He took away the binding around her skull. Her hair had begun to grow, short and thick like a boy's. It had been fair when they shaved her head, now it was black. Linli looked at Dr Lascaux in horror.

"Go on," Lascaux instructed as if nothing was wrong. "Take the pads away."

Linli removed the pads from her eyes. They were closed and her lashes were dark. She lay back against the pillows, calm and remote, as if there was nothing wrong with her, as if she was unaware that this moment could mean the difference between life and death.

"Open your eyes, Andra," Lascaux instructed.

She obeyed him. In the dim room her eyes were

staring at him, no longer blue but dark and unfathomable.

Lascaux recoiled. What had he done? What had he done to her? Changed her hair from white-fair to black. Changed her eyes from blue to . . . brown? Changed her from a normal person into a freak, an oddity, like Kiroyo. Kiroyo's eyes were brown and he was an oddity. Her eyes were big in her small pointed face. Lascaux stared at her and felt his repulsion go. She was not an oddity. She was Andra!

He switched on a tiny torch.

"Andra, can you see?"

Her eyes moved to the light.

"That? Yes. I can see it. I can see you too. You're going bald and there are a pair of scissors and a thermometer in your coat pocket. I can see Linli. Linli, you are ugly and you have a squint."

Lascaux heaved a sigh of relief. She was not blind. He would not have to expire her. She could see.

Andra glanced round the room.

"What a dull, uninteresting place this is," she said. "I had hoped it would be different. Just flat walls. No window to let in the sun. No sky. Just the ceiling and the blue light which changes to white at the flick of a switch. The colours are dead, not alive. There is nothing alive, only us."

The door opened suddenly, letting in a flood of bright light. An old man stood there. His brown eyes behind his spectacles eyed the scene with

52

distaste. His hair was turning grey. His tunic was silver and on his collar was a gold badge. Who was this important old man who leant on a metal cane and surveyed them?

"Shut that door," Lascaux snapped.

The door shut and the pain went from Andra's eyes. She saw now just a soft impression of a person standing at the end of her bed.

"I have come for my injection," the old man said. "They told me where to find you."

Lascaux was watching Andra; her reactions to the sudden changes of light intensity.

"You should have knocked." He looked up. "Professor Kiroyo, my old friend, I did not know it was you."

Andra hugged her knees. So that's who he was. The great Professor Kiroyo, the oldest man alive. Three hundred years old. Everyone had heard of Professor Kiroyo.

"This is Linli, one of my students," Lascaux told the old man. "And this is Andra."

Kiroyo favoured her with a brief nod. He did not like young people.

"Lascaux," Kiroyo said, "if it's not troubling you too much, I would like my injection now. I am extremely busy and if it had not been for a meeting with Shenlyn I should not be here."

"Of course," Lascaux murmured. "I will come with you now. Linli, bind Andra's eyes."

They turned to go.

"No!" Andra said. "I don't want my eyes covered."

Lascaux threw an apologetic glance to Kiroyo and said to her:

"You must not strain your eyes, Andra. You must use them only for short periods until they are stronger. The pads can come off again tomorrow."

The old man moved forward and clutched the rail of the bed. He stared at the girl with renewed interest. He had been told that Lascaux had performed a brain graft. This must be the girl. He gazed at her white pointed face and realised that her eyes were brown like his own. What a pity she would never see the things he had seen and never know what he knew. Or maybe it was better that way. She was happy, but if she knew what they had lost she would be sad. Everything gone in a moment of time, and she did not even know. No one really knew but himself.

"What did you say her name was?" Kiroyo asked.

"Andra," said Lascaux.

KIROYO

6

The library was silent except for the whirr of the computer which was never silent. Kiroyo selected a book at random, then swung his chair back to the desk. Carefully he turned the brittle yellow pages, vainly searching for some small fact. He ran his fingers through his greying hair. For a moment he could not even remember what he was looking for. His concentration was not as keen as it used to be.

His eyes left the book and surveyed the girl who sat by the computer. He frowned. How long was it since she had touched the machine? Sixty minutes? More? He should reprimand her but he was reluctant to disturb her composure. Her eyes darted across the page and she smiled to herself as she read. She was strange, this sixteen-year-old girl they had sent him from EDCO four months ago. He was used to working on his own. He was alarmed when Shenlyn insisted he have an assistant, but now he was glad she was here.

He studied her pale pointed face, which was now frowning. There was something in the book she did not understand. She raised her eyes and they were questioning. He nodded to her and she began to read. Her voice was low and husky. She did not talk with the dull monotone of most people. She read as if she saw what she read, she gave her words expression and he listened with pleasure.

"What a still, hot, perfect day! What a golden desert this spreading moor! Everywhere sunshine. I wished I could live in it and on it. I saw a lizard run over the crags; I saw a bee busy among the bilberries! What are bilberries, Professor Kiroyo?"

"A small black single fruit of a thornless plant. In our country they called them blueberries. Do you know what a bee is?"

"Of course! It was the flying insect they used to pollinate the flowers. Their colouring was usually yellow and brown. They had multiple eyes and converted nectar to honey. They were composed of a head, thorax and abdomen, six legs and a sting. They made a low humming noise."

"Very good. And a lizard?"

"A small reptile similar in shape to a crocodile. The English lizards were non-ferocious."

Kiroyo nodded his head and she returned to the book. The books she chose were very different from his. When she could she read fiction, for in fiction she told him there were many facts. And yet he felt disturbed. That child enjoyed reading too much. She did not regard it as work and she was forgetting to feed what facts she obtained into the computer. But how quickly she was learning!

58

It was as if she had known it all before and was simply refreshing her memory.

He waited another fifteen minutes, and still she had not touched the machine.

"Andra," Kiroyo said. "What book are you reading?"

"*Jane Eyre*."

He believed it had been a classic but the setting escaped him.

"I do not think I know it. Is it informative?"

"Not very," she said. "It is set before the age of machines. The people used candles and their conveyances were pulled by the horse."

Kiroyo was annoyed. How many times had he told her? Ten? Twenty? Dickens, Austen, even Shakespeare, she had read before he had realised she was wasting her labour time. He sighed. He supposed he must tell her yet again.

"Why do you read it then? No useful facts can be taken from such a book."

She scowled at him. They had sent Andra to him because she did not conform. They did not want her rebellious nature to disturb the working community. They had told him her IQ was average. Kiroyo had found out they were wrong. She had character, personality and intelligence, and by her scowl she showed she had some spirit. But even Andra would not yet defy so distinguished a person as Professor Kiroyo.

"Why do you read that book?" Kiroyo asked again.

Her hands gripped the edge of her chair. He could see the whiteness of her knuckles. She wanted to answer him, but still she hesitated.

"You may speak your mind," Kiroyo prompted her.

It was an opportunity Andra could not let pass. Her dark eyes flashed.

"I read it because I want to read it. You heard it. You heard the flow of the words. This isn't just a language, it's beautiful. The things in these books are beautiful, but in this whole horrible subterranean place there is nothing, not one thing, I would class as beautiful. The language we speak is empty and void of any real meaning. Beauty no longer exists."

He stared at her, at the flush of pink which tinged her cheeks, then faded, leaving them white. She looked nervous. Was she afraid the wrath of the great Kiroyo would strike her down? He had asked her to speak her mind. He could not be angry because she had obeyed him.

Kiroyo sighed.

"Andra, you are here to work. We want facts, my dear, not fiction. Shenlyn requires every available fact we have concerning life on the surface of the earth two thousand years ago. But he does not want to know about the age before machines, that is a little too barbaric. Facts are what Shenlyn requires, Andra. Facts, facts and more facts, not fairy stories."

Andra sniffed.

Kiroyo took off his glasses and breathed on them. What! Would she answer him back yet again?

"This book is not entirely factless. I have learnt that a field is an agricultural division. That hay is dried grass and is used for feeding ruminants during the winter. I have learnt that wood is combustible, it will kindle to flame which gives warmth in the cold. I have learnt that wood comes from trees and that trees are perennial plants with a woody stem dividing to branches, twigs and leaves. I have never seen a tree, but Charlotte Brontë has described it so accurately that I feel that if ever I should meet one I would recognise it as a tree and be able to distinguish it from a bilberry, a bee, or a small English lizard."

Hers was a rich scorn. She turned to the computer and pounded the keyboard furiously. The knobs hissed and the great machine whirred and clicked and seemed to tremble under the relentless driving of her hands. Kiroyo chuckled. She was a gem, this child raw from EDCO. He was glad Shenlyn had demanded he have an assistant.

She swung from the machine to face him.

"Your scorn is a refreshing change," the old man said calmly, and almost indifferently thumbing through the pages of his book. "I am glad you are capable of thinking for yourself and are not one of the countless duplicated minds EDCO is so skilled in producing. You are not entirely dependent on me or the computer. Good! I have observed that your understanding of the English language is excellent. In time you may come to understand it even better than I who have studied it all my life."

Andra was still not satisfied. She was no longer afraid of this silent old man whose knowledge had at first filled her with awe. She was learning all the time. She was learning about all the things she already knew. The pictures in her mind she could now name. She felt she was almost on a level with Kiroyo. She would not be afraid to talk to him for he was not so very different from Dr Lascaux.

"And how long is all your life, Kiroyo?" she asked. "Over three hundred years, isn't it? You should be dead. I should hate to be compelled to live so long in this dreary sunless city."

Her words demanded Kiroyo's attention. She had not called him by his proper title. He was no longer Professor Kiroyo, but simply Kiroyo. The old man was not sure he liked the familiarity. He looked up from his book. She was gazing at the ceiling so high above, where the whiteness glowed from every part to give them heat and light. Her lips curled in scorn.

Kiroyo said:

"It's the best we can offer you. The surface of the earth is no longer habitable."

He regarded her grim features. Not long ago, lost in her book, he had thought her pretty. Now her small face was pinched and her large brown eyes were unsmiling. He wondered why she always wore a cap.

"I know," Andra said. "I know, because two thousand years ago we destroyed it. We, with our great machines, destroyed every living thing and condemned ourselves to creep like worms beneath the surface. My ancestors made me worse than a slug, never to see a tree or a flower growing under the sky, never to feel the wind, or the rain, or see the sun. To crawl through these metal passages where even the air we breathe is manufactured and the food we eat is synthetic, and words have no meaning. There is no love, no hope, no happiness. This is not living, Kiroyo. This is merely existing, being kept alive to keep our species alive and feed the demands of Shenlyn and the computers."

Kiroyo was startled.

"You are very bitter, Andra."

Still she gazed at the ceiling, watching the whiteness which constantly glowed but never flickered, light which gave them warmth but was not warm. Kiroyo stared at her. Her sorrow reached out across the vastness of the room and he felt its intensity. She was very young and her feelings were the violence of youth. He, who was old, had learnt to accept.

"If you are bitter, Andra, it will not help. The world you read of is gone and no bitterness can make it return."

She did not seem to see or hear him. The white ceiling held her eyes.

"I want to see the sun again," she said. "With every breath I take I long to see the sun. It's like a pain inside me. I saw it once, long ago. There were mountains, very high, reaching against the sky and peaked with snow. It sank behind them and the whole sky was pink, rose, orange and scarlet. It made me want to paint. I tried, but I couldn't capture it, the luminous quality, the huge shining vastness of the sky. God! It was so great it took my breath away."

"Andra," Kiroyo said. "You talk like a fool! You imagine and think you have seen. Here is Darwin's *Theory of Evolution*. Read it!"

She came and took the book from his hand. The binding was dull blue.

She said coolly:

"Everything is different now. The Earth revolves round the Sun on a different orbit. Time has a different meaning. It takes four years to swing once round the Sun. Four years: eight seasons: two winters, two springs, two summers, two autumns: eight multiplied by six months is four long weary years. So far from the Sun it goes that the whole surface is frozen: that is spring, and autumn, and winter. In the summer it comes a little nearer, enough to melt some of the ice and snow and allow a trickle of water to run down a mountain-side, to collect as a stream, merge with other streams and flow as a river down to the freezing sea. That is the Earth now: so cold that nothing can live up there and only we, so far below the heavy rocks, live on in this warm and skyless city and are not even aware of the changing elements above us. I damn the man who dropped that bomb! Back through two thousand years of time I damn him! He swung the Earth from her orbit just to end one stupid war and left us with a lump of useless rock."

Andra tucked a stray end of hair into her cap.

"Is there a guitar in the museum, Kiroyo?"

Guitar? How the child's mind roamed from subject to subject. Guitar?

"A stringed instrument," she prompted him. "They were popular in the years immediately before we came underground. They make pleasant music."

"There are several guitars in the museum. There is a machine in there which reproduces the sounds they made . . . a revolving black disc called the 'Winds of Hawaii'. One day I will let you hear it. But why do you ask?"

She smiled to herself.

"Syrd plays the vinet. He plays well, but the vinet has no depth, no feeling, and no soul. I would love to hear Syrd play the guitar."

Kiroyo said:

"The things in the museum are very valuable and quite irreplaceable, and that includes the guitars."

He hoped she understood his meaning. She

opened the book he had given her and began to read. Her forehead crinkled with distaste. Kiroyo stared at her. He was trying to remember . . . a guitar? Dr Lascaux had asked him about a guitar when he had gone for his last rejuvenating injection. There had been a girl on a bed in a room with green walls. She had had a brain graft and her eyes had been dark. Kiroyo stared intently at Andra and he remembered.

7

Every morning at 0600 hours when the blue light of night was turned to white daylight, Kiroyo left his solitary apartment in the upper social sector of the city to seek the familiar quietness of the archives. It was a walk of two miles, for the archives were situated on the outskirts. There he would study for two or maybe three hours until his eyes began to stray to the clock and his ears strain for the sound of her footsteps in the passage outside. The pearled glass doors would swing open and she would be there: Andra, white-skinned, dark-eyed, with her silver swirling cloak and short tunic. Every day she was different: sometimes happy, sometimes sad, sometimes pensive, sometimes talkative, but always he was glad when she came.

"Bah!" thought Kiroyo. "I grow soft in the head waiting for Andra to make my day begin."

Today she was in high spirits. She was singing whilst she searched the shelves for the book she wanted. The old man found himself humming the tune. He wondered what the word Omyara meant. He would ask Andra. She shared an apartment with Syrd, and it was Syrd who had made the song. It was Syrd whose pictures hung on the walls of the main street and caused the working girls to scream at the mention of his name. It was a catchy tune. Shenlyn himself had been singing it last night and Kiroyo had laughed at him. But Shenlyn had merely shrugged and said: "Well, can I not sing the song the young people sing and let my age slip away for a while? The young ones worship the ground he walks on. To them he is a God and it is all a very harmless adoration. I, Shenlyn, do not mind if he steals some of my glory." Shenlyn had been in a remarkably good humour last night.

Kiroyo listened to the words Andra sang:

"I run through metal roads
And through the curving passages of time.
Omyara, take me in;
Let me sink into the darkness that is you."

"Andra?" Kiroyo asked when she had finished. "What does it mean?"

"Does it matter?" she replied. "Kiroyo, can I listen to their music from the museum? Once you said you would let me hear it, those little black discs and the square box. Can I hear it now?"

Kiroyo tried to be firm.

"Music is not essential to life, Andra. We must not waste time. Shenlyn demands that we work."

"Oh, pot to Shenlyn!"

She used such crude archaic expressions. He would not give in to her, not this time. He had let her play the guitar once, but he would not give in again. She did not realise how important their work was. They might be working with things of the past, but they were still working for the future. He, Kiroyo, knew what they were working for, but Andra did not. Now she wanted music and there was no time for music. He took the keys from the drawer of his desk.

"Go and get it," he said, and threw them to her.

She caught the flash of metal and jangled them in her hand.

"The largest one. And Andra . . ."

"Yes, Kiroyo?"

"If you break one of those little black discs, my dear, I shall have you immediately transferred to the protein processing laboratory."

"Kiroyo, do not be such a stuffed shirt," she said. "And thank you. We used to sing carols in the streets. It was dark and sometimes there was snow so we took lanterns. Maybe fifteen or twenty of us would go. We went round all the houses and we never got home before midnight. It was Christmas morning when we went to bed. It's sad there's no Christmas now."

The door to the museum swung open and she was gone, leaving Kiroyo worried behind her. There was something wrong with Andra, something wrong with her mind. She went back through two thousand years of time and told of events as if she actually remembered them. He ought to tell Lascaux. He ought to have told him

69

long ago, when he had first noticed. But if he told Lascaux maybe they would take her away, break her spirit, rehabilitate her, destroy her. He didn't want that to happen. The archives would be empty without Andra and he would be a lonely old man. He would rather remain silent and let her stay.

He drummed his fingers on the desk top. She came from the museum. In her arms she carried the record-player and she was smiling at him.

"Soon we shall have a party, Kiroyo. Syrd, Daëmon and I. It will be a marvellous party, Kiroyo, full of surprises. Will you come?"

"Am I not too old, Andra? Do you young things want an old man of 306 years of age intruding in your fun?"

"You are only 290 years older than me and it will do your poor rheumaticky limbs good to dance. You will dance with me, Papa Kiroyo."

"No! No! No! Andra! There is no disease now. My limbs are quite healthy or I would not be here."

"Of course not, I was forgetting. I was thinking of another old man. He had rheumatism. His hands were just like claws all shrivelled up. He used to sit close to the fire, or by the window when it was sunny. The sun used to come mottled with green through the trees and splashed like yellow flowers. That old man smelt of tweed and tobacco. It was he who taught me to play. No one played like him. He made the guitar himself and its music was like the soul of the mountains and . . ."

"Andra!" Kiroyo shouted. "Andra, stop it! Stop it now!"

This child, she should not be here. Lascaux should have her, not me. Her mind wandered and she could no longer distinguish between the real and the imaginary.

She looked at him in surprise.

"Was I forgetting again? I shall have to try harder. It used to scare me at first until I got used to it. I've just accepted it now. It's not the books which put these pictures in my head, it's something else, someone else. His name is Richard Carson. Dr Lascaux said he doesn't exist but he does."

Kiroyo shook his head.

"I am not sure I understand you, Andra."

She smiled.

"We work well together, don't we? You are a professor of ancient English. I am an artist of ancient English. I paint the pictures and you analyse them, but at the same time you lean back and admire them. I go back through time and take you with me and you are not unhappy to come. You would not send me away, Papa Kiroyo?"

Kiroyo patted her hand.

"Papa Kiroyo! Bah! I should spank you. You say these things to deliberately confuse me and then you laugh. Papa Kiroyo indeed!

"No, I will not send you away."

"And you will come to our party and dance with me? No! We will not wait for the party. Come tonight! Come tonight and have supper with us. Come and see our room. Kiroyo, there is something in our room you ought to see, I want you to see, even though I hide it away. I don't understand myself any more, but maybe you will. You will come, Papa Kiroyo?"

The old man shook his head again.

"Tonight I am meeting Shenlyn and Renson for a social evening. Tomorrow evening I am giving one of my rare lectures at EDCO to the students of geology. The evening after I go to have my hair trimmed."

She stamped her foot.

"You mean old man! You would rather meet Shenlyn than come home with me? You could meet Syrd and Syrd is far more important than Shenlyn. Most people would give their lives for an evening with Syrd. Do you know, I don't like Shenlyn. He is ugly."

"How do you know, Andra? Have you met Shenlyn? I thought he seldom left his suite at Administration."

"He just sounds ugly," Andra said. "And you are coming to supper with me, Kiroyo, three evenings from now. Now can I play the music?"

She did not wait for his permission. She opened the lid.

"How does it work?"

Kiroyo plugged it in, took the black disc from

her hand, put it on the turntable and dropped the needle upon it with a practised hand. She watched him with her head on one side and her eyes bright like the pictures of birds he had seen. Pictures! Soon he would show Andra the pictures, all the books locked in the case he would show her. She would see the animals, the birds, the plants, the colours of the earth two thousand years ago. And when she saw them and realised that all that remained was grey ruins under the grey sky then she would have cause to be bitter.

The library was filled with sudden sound, primitive instruments they had never heard before. Andra swayed in the centre of the floor, caught up in the surge of savage music. A strand of hair escaped from her cap and hung long and black. Kiroyo stared at it.

The music faded away, leaving only an echo. She clapped her hands in delight.

"It was marvellous, Kiroyo. The beat, the music! Marvellous! Can I play it again?"

"Andra," Kiroyo said, "take off your cap."

She stared at him and her wild dancing ceased.

"No."

"Take it off, Andra."

Her brown eyes were rebellious and defiant. Then she snatched the cap from her head and her hair fell past her shoulders in gentle waves, black as the night sky that sported the stars. Her look was challenging.

"You naughty girl. You silly, silly child. Why?"

"It's my hair."

"But it's long, Andra. No one has long hair. It's not allowed. It's not civilised."

She piled it back in her cap.

"It's my hair," she repeated. "And it's staying long. I like it like that."

"Then be careful no one sees."

"No one has," she said. "Only you, Papa Kiroyo, and you would not tell."

She reached out for the record to play it again. Then she stopped and stared around the room.

"Is something wrong, Andra?"

She looked at him.

"Something is about to happen, Papa Kiroyo. Something wonderful and something terrible is beginning now. Hold still, Papa Kiroyo; hold still and listen."

The old man held his breath. There was a moment of tense silence then the microphone blared. The loud voice from Administration hurt his ears.

"Personnel will remain where they are for an immediate security check."

Andra closed the lid of the record player and settled herself beside the computer.

"I do not ever remember a security check," she said.

"There has not been one for over a hundred years."

8

Kiroyo sipped the sweet liquid and gazed over the glass at the tall, broad-shouldered man in the pale blue uniform. "He should have been an athlete," Kiroyo thought. His muscles were firm and his face was unmarred by the wrinkles of age. He was tall, well over six feet, and his deep gold hair straggled over his eyes. He looked like a young man and yet Kiroyo knew he was nearing his second century. How uninspiring Renson seemed beside Shenlyn. He must be fifty years younger but he looked years older. He was small and portly and losing his hair. The dome of his skull was bald and shiny and his face wore a perpetual worried frown.

Cromer was lounging in an easy chair, his purple-stockinged feet thrust on to a footstool. He looked perfectly at ease. His hard blue eyes were quite expressionless, but he was smiling sardonically at Shenlyn pacing the room, brows drawn together to scowl at the gold and green carpet. Cromer was the essence of calm, but something had certainly disturbed Shenlyn.

"For heaven's sake sit down," Cromer said at last. "You are making my legs ache."

Kiroyo did not like the younger man. He

always seemed so cocksure of himself. Maybe he had reason to be: was he not head of the security department? Had he not received the gold badge? He was just in his thirtieth year and at the top of the ladder. Only Shenlyn was above him. But Kiroyo still did not like him. He simply oozed with conceit, did that man with the glowing purple uniform.

The old man forced himself to ask of Cromer:

"What was it all about?"

Cromer's eyes flashed with anger at Kiroyo's uninterested attitude. Then he shrugged.

"The plans of the big computer are missing."

"Is that all?"

Renson said:

"It was the rocket computer. We only found out by chance. Cromer thought he would have one of his annual check-ups in the technical file room, went through the blueprints and found it missing. It could have been taken months ago."

"Are you sure it is not simply mislaid?"

Cromer said:

"We do not mislay important information, Kiroyo."

"But surely such a small thing does not warrant a general security check?"

Shenlyn growled:

"Normally, no. But you see, Kiroyo, my old friend, the ship is due to land within the next month."

Kiroyo raised an eyebrow.

"So soon? You did not tell me."

"Fenner gave her an extra burst of speed. She will be here in twenty-seven days. Not many know, but even the tightest security can leak. There are little gaps which become regrettable, are there not, Cromer?"

Renson chuckled.

"Our friend Cromer had reason to look sour. This security check brought something else to light. We found an infiltrator working on the rocket site. His name was Buven. We found another in the mechanical workshop which is responsible for several components of our fleet. His name was Alexen. Now do you see, Kiroyo, why Shenlyn is uneasy?"

"Infiltrators from Uralia? But how did they get through the security men on the entrance to the highway?"

"We have no idea," Cromer said calmly. "As Shenlyn said: there is a little leak in security which is regrettable. Even *I* am not infallible."

Shenlyn glowered at him.

"You will need to be infallible from now on, Cromer. I want those plans found. That ship relies on the computer to bring her down. If anything goes wrong she won't make it and she's *got* to make it."

"She has," Kiroyo murmured. "Yes, she must make it."

"You know a Uralian ship landed yesterday?" Cromer inquired.

"I know," said Shenlyn. "And ours is landing in twenty-seven days' time. If anything goes wrong I shall be out for your guts, Cromer."

"I do not see why you are so het up, Shenlyn," Cromer remarked. "The chances that the Uralian ship has also found 801 are microscopic, and there is nothing wrong with the computer, I've had it checked. Even Grovinski would not be so stupid as to try to prevent our ship from landing. Why should he? If the Uralians have taken the plans they probably only think our computer is more efficient than theirs and want one like it."

"I am not familiar with the intimate workings of Commandant Grovinski's mind, Cromer. All I know is that the plans are missing and our ship is due to land. If you have to undo every screw in Sub-city One, I want them found. Cromer, I want them found!"

Cromer struggled to his feet and thrust his legs into his black shiny boots. The gold badge on his collar glittered as it caught the light.

"I can see that you are in no mood to conduct a pleasant social evening, Shenlyn. I will find my own entertainment. You'll have my report in the morning."

The head of security strode away. Kiroyo felt an immediate easing of the tension.

"Surely," he said, "you do not seriously think Grovinski would stoop so low? As Cromer said: the chances that their ship has found planet 801 are practically non-existent."

Shenlyn looked grim.

"I admit the chance is remote, but I can afford to take *no* chance. The ships will be ready to leave in twelve months' time."

"A year!"

Kiroyo was startled. He had known Shenlyn's intentions but he had thought five years at the earliest.

"You are a dark horse, Shenlyn. You plan a huge evacuation of our Sub-cities and you tell no one. I tell you it is too soon."

Shenlyn shook his head.

"Too soon cannot be soon enough. This earth cannot support us for more than a couple of centuries. We must all be gone by then. We have drained her dry. The vital minerals are in short supply. We have to leave, and the sooner the better."

"You'll never be ready. You'll be sending those people there to die. They don't know how to live on the surface and 801 may not be all you think. Surely it is too soon to set your heart on this thing? But I see you have. I wish you luck and I'm glad it's your headache, not mine."

"It's also your headache," Renson reminded Kiroyo. "Shenlyn asked me to get on to you several days ago. We are not receiving enough material from your computer."

Shenlyn towered over the old man.

"You are not working efficiently, Kiroyo. Why, I even sent you an assistant. We want facts down to the smallest detail. 801 is, as far as we know, identical to this earth as it used to be. I don't intend to send those people to their deaths; I intend them to live. But they will have to know how to live. You have not started on medical data and Linli has graduated to receive it. You are falling behind, old man."

Kiroyo nodded his head. He was not surprised to hear that. Andra would have to put away her music and stop wasting their time. Shenlyn himself was displeased.

Renson murmured:

"You find it difficult to work with a young girl, Kiroyo, after being so long on your own?"

"Damn difficult!" Kiroyo agreed.

"It was Dr Lascaux's work of art they sent you, was it not?"

"Eh?" queried Shenlyn.

"The girl EDCO sent to the archives to assist Kiroyo, the one on whom Dr Lascaux performed his brain graft. Don't you remember?"

"Vaguely. You must work the girl harder, Kiroyo. You were working more efficiently on your own. Is her IQ low?"

"Oh no," Kiroyo protested. "Her IQ is not low. I would grade her at 145. She knows more than I do."

"145!" said Renson in amazement. "Surely not. If she had been that brilliant she would be here in Administration."

"She is 145 in my department but she would

only be 95 in Administration. And anyway, she does not like you, Shenlyn."

Shenlyn looked surprised.

"Why not?"

"She says you sound ugly. The expression she uses is: Pot to Shenlyn."

Renson laughed. Shenlyn scowled and said:

"You make fun of me, old man. Keep that girl of yours out of my way, or maybe she will find that I *am* ugly. She is an insolent young madam. What is her name?"

"Andra," said Kiroyo.

9

Andra tucked her arm through Kiroyo's as they walked towards the centre of the city. They paused for a moment at the entrance to the arterial highway whilst Kiroyo passed a few cordial remarks with the patrol men. Andra peered along its straightness, along the curving, ill-lit walls until it disappeared into a blob of light. She saw a car speeding along to turn off into one of the subsidiary tunnels. She had always wanted to go along there, along the vast lighted road which led to the two other Sub-cities and the five cities of Uralia. Sixteen thousand miles it went below the surface of the earth. It wasn't to the cities that Andra wanted to go, not to the mines, the power station, or the nuclear generators, but to the sea gardens. She could imagine them deep on the ocean floor where men worked with fish and flew like birds in the air. It seemed to Andra that working in the sea gardens must be a kind of freedom, almost as good as going above.

"I would like to go to the sea gardens," she told Kiroyo.

The old man grunted. He was tired. The archives were a long way from the centre. He should ask Shenlyn for a car, but that would be admitting he was feeling his age. The past weeks had taken the last of his energy. They had worked from the beginning of daylight right round to dark. His mind was whirring like the computer but it seemed that Andra had survived well enough.

Her brown eyes regarded him seriously.

"You look a tired old man, Papa Kiroyo. Your feet shuffle and your eyelids droop. Come and sit with Andra in the gardens for a while."

She led him away from Administration Square round the back of the buildings where the gardens were. There she sat him on the wall round the lake and he could see the fish which drifted with peaceful unconcern and shining unblinking eyes. The fish had come from the deep sea where Andra wanted to go. He found their movements soothing.

Andra tucked a loose strand of hair into her cap and picked a flower from a bush. She moved its petals with her long white fingers, then crushed it and threw it into the water.

"You destructive child."

"That is not a real flower. That is a pathetic attempt at one. Its petals are brittle and its colours harsh. It has no softness and no scent. It cannot even reproduce itself without men to transfer its pollen. Look at this place. This is all that is left of the wild growing things men once had, these few pitiful specimens. Five miles above them is the sun and they've never seen it."

She was staring up at the roof, but it was too high above even for Andra to see, just the glowing light that was not the sun. It was too white and too constant to be the sun, and too cool. As she watched, the light dimmed to blue. The hours of darkness had begun: 2000 until 0600, ten hours of darkness, fourteen hours of light: light without the sun, dark without the moon and stars.

Andra bent her head.

"It makes me want to cry. There is no wind, no rain, no air. The roof comes lower and lower and shuts me in. I can't breathe and the ache inside me hurts like a pain. Kiroyo, will I ever see the sun?"

Kiroyo straightened his aching back. Andra was all wrong. How could she possibly know what they had lost? How could she long for something she had never seen? But he knew how she felt. He had seen the sky and he never passed an opportunity to see it again.

"Next time there is an expedition to the surface I will take you with me, Andra. I will show you that sun you so desire to see. And now, my dear, shall we go and have this supper you promised me? We should not be here in the gardens after the hours of darkness."

She took his hand and she was smiling.

"But you are the great Professor Kiroyo. Such little rules do not apply to you."

Kiroyo heard his footsteps echo on the metal road.

"And it seems, Andra, they do not apply to you

either. Does any rule apply to you? Your hair is long and your thoughts, I have no doubt, are rebellious. You defy Shenlyn in front of his very nose. I sincerely hope, Andra, that you and Shenlyn never meet."

Andra laughed, then became serious.

"Pot to Shenlyn," she said.

SYRD

10

Syrd was impatient. His fingers plucked restlessly at the strings of his vinet, producing neither harmony nor melody. Daëmon hummed as he laid out the meal. His cheerfulness annoyed Syrd. The bright geometrical frescoes he himself had painted covered every part of the walls and made his eyes ache. The colours were harsh, the designs too symmetrical. He disliked them and knew Andra did too, but she insisted on their being there to cover her own strange paintings.

Where was Andra? She was late again. Every evening this week she had been late. She was bringing someone to supper and she ought not to be late. He wondered who it was and if they had called in at the youth centre on their way. He strummed idly. His fingers ached to play the guitar Andra had hidden under her bed.

"Play something definite," Daëmon said, "Omyara."

No, he would not sing. He was thinking of Andra. Why did she always wear a cap? Was it because her hair was black and she was ashamed? Syrd had seen her hair once, not long after Dr Lascaux had taken away the bandages. It was very short, not pretty hair, but nothing to be ashamed of. He struck a vicious chord and the vinet clattered to the floor. The music of the vinet had no soul, the guitar sighed and vibrated with a special kind of magic. It made a beautiful sound and he could play it better than Andra or Daëmon.

Syrd picked up the weekly news-sheet and a biscuit. It was hard and dry. Andra was an appalling cook.

"You haven't put your dirty tunic in the bin," Daëmon said. "The woman comes tomorrow to collect the washing."

"I know. I will remember in the morning. It's on the floor of my room."

Daëmon retrieved the vinet and propped it against the wall.

"You are worse than a woman," Syrd commented.

"Someone has to keep the apartment tidy. You and Andra never clear up your rubbish and we have a guest for supper."

"Who is it?" Syrd asked.

"I have no idea. Maeia, maybe. If you're not reading the news-sheet, may I have it?"

Syrd held it out and blew the crumbs from his tunic.

Everyone thought he was a God. His photographs hung on the walls of the buildings, his song was played over the microphones, everyone knew his name, men sang his song on the way to work, girls screamed and clawed at him when he sang at the youth centre. He was Syrd who had made Omyara. Everyone worshipped him but Andra.

He had never known anyone like Andra, never known anyone who talked like her, never been so deeply moved by spoken words before. He had come here for a reason, but Andra made that reason unimportant. She made him forget Uralia and all it stood for. He was filled with dissatisfaction, roused to anger by the things she said. He was being caught up in her useless revolution against the conditions in Sub-city One, and Sub-city One was not his city. He was merely here to work . . . for Grovinski . . . and how often Andra made him forget.

"Dr Lascaux is visiting Petrov to discuss the technicalities of a brain transplant," Daëmon said.

"Is he?"

"Dr Linli has qualified and a woman has given birth to quadruplets, three of whom have been expired as physically defective."

"Oh yes?"

"Shenlyn is calling a meeting of the Directors of the three Sub-cities. There's a review of Fynn's new drama. Do you want to hear it?"

"No," Syrd said crossly. "What is she planning?"

Daëmon's brilliant blue eyes left the news-sheet.

"Who?"

"Andra! She's using us. You and me. The kids

at the youth centre. She's heading for trouble and taking us with her."

"Would that be so terrible? I never realised there was anything wrong with our way of life until Andra told us. We're not people any more, Syrd, we're robots. We do just what we're told, think what we're told, and go where we're told. It's time something happened. It's time something changed."

"I didn't come here to find trouble," Syrd said.

Daëmon shrugged and went back to his reading.

Syrd brooded at the wall. He hadn't come to find trouble, to be part of Andra's uprising. He had come to serve Grovinski. If Cromer knew what Andra was doing the security of Sub-city One would be focused on this apartment. They would be watched continually, he, Daëmon and Andra. He had been accepted as a citizen here, given a position at the space centre working with the computers. Outwardly he was just another member of the community, inwardly a Uralian agent, and that's the way he had to stay. No one knew about the ashes of the blueprints in the kitchen incinerator. But if Andra brought security here they could find out even now. It would be so much easier if he hated Andra, so much easier to destroy her.

"This should interest you," Daëmon said. "A Uralian space ship landed seven days ago."

"Why do you think I should be interested?"

"Well, you did come from there. It's news from home."

"I may have been born there but I'm not Uralian any more. The computer proved that. I am the same nationality as you. Salynka was a hell-hole anyway."

"So you don't want me to read it to you?"

Syrd reached for the vinet. The waiting was making him edgy, pulling his nerves taut. Every minute of the day was an act, saying the right lines at the right time, never giving himself away. And all the time there was Andra. If she had been one of the ordinary blue-eyed dimwits from EDCO, it wouldn't have mattered. But she was sharp. Her eyes missed nothing and could see further than any other eyes. Andra would notice an expression on his face which would give himself away. Andra would notice a reaction which was wrong. Maybe Andra already knew why he was here.

"Read it," Syrd said.

Daëmon read:

"'The Uralian space ship, Cvmrokov, landed seven days ago in the vicinity of Petrov. It was known to have been carrying a crew of thirty-five men. Our scientists are uncertain where the ship had been but state that it had been away for at least seventy-five years. Grovinski has ordered a day of festivities to welcome the astronauts home.' Did you know they found two infiltrators from Uralia during the security check?"

"I had heard," Syrd said.

Daëmon regarded him thoughtfully. Syrd felt uneasy.

"Why are you staring at me? I'm not an infiltrator. I came here openly. They know I'm here. Cromer, Shenlyn. I spent weeks in therapy, weeks with that computer. How many times must I tell you I'm not Uralian any more? I'm just the same as you and I'll thank you not to forget it."

"Sorry," Daëmon said. "You jumped to the wrong conclusion, my friend. I was just thinking it was an odd coincidence: their ship landing, our computer plans missing, two of their agents being found and our own ship coming down in less than a month."

"Less than a month?"

"Fenner gave her a burst of speed."

Syrd played the introduction to his song. Less than a month. He'd been here nine already. In nine months he had become part of the routine function of the city. He came and went through the main computer room and no one even noticed him now. Less than a month was more than enough time to destroy the ship before she came to earth.

"Yes, it is odd," Syrd agreed. "Coincidence is always odd."

He started to sing:

"Omyara: you come whirling patterns in my mind.

You call through my dreams with echoes that
    run
Like my footsteps that come
Far behind you.
As through the curving passages of time
I chase to find you . . ."

The door handle turned. Andra was here. Syrd
stiffened and stopped playing. The time had come
to start another act, to watch his words and guard
his thoughts from Andra's eyes. She came into the
room, smiled at him and stood aside.

A man shuffled in. His hair was greying and his
shoulders drooped. He wore old-fashioned spectacles instead of contact lenses. Syrd knew who he
was. He rose to his feet. Why had Andra brought
him here? How had she persuaded him to come?
How had she dared to ask him to lower his social
position and enter the apartments of commoners?
Syrd glanced swiftly round the room. Thank
goodness Daëmon had made it tidy. He kicked
the news-sheet under the divan. Damn Andra!
Why did she have to bring that old man here?

Her dark eyes glowed with laughter and her
silver tunic reflected the light. Syrd stood awk-
wardly as she took the old man's cloak.

"Syrd," Andra said, "this is Papa Kiroyo."

Papa Kiroyo? Surely he should be Professor
Kiroyo? Syrd held out his hand. Kiroyo took it.
His grip was firm, not shaky like an old man.

"Professor Kiroyo, it is good to know you," Syrd said correctly.

The old man smiled.

"So you are Syrd. I am out of touch with most things, but even *I* recognise you. I have seen your photographs in the street. I even know your song. Andra sings it. So does Shenlyn. I do not think he had the words right but it was a brave try. Tell me, young man, what this word Omyara means."

Syrd returned an automatic smile. He had never spoken to such an old man before. Just once to Shenlyn and even Shenlyn was a hundred years younger than Kiroyo. Syrd saw the shining gold badge on Kiroyo's collar and answered respectfully:

"I do not know. Maybe it is someone's name or maybe it is something which has no name and no existence. I just made it up. Omyara: it is a pretty lucky word."

He hoped Andra would not ask him to play, not before Kiroyo. To him his music would seem like the rattle of a baby's toy. Why had she brought Kiroyo here?

"And this is Daëmon," Andra said.

Daëmon bowed.

"He, too, is an important person, Papa Kiroyo. He is the leader of the young people and he works in the space centre. Daëmon, what have you cooked? Kiroyo and I are starving. The meals they bring us in the archives are always cold; it is so far away. Daëmon does our cooking, Papa Kiroyo, they do not like the meals I make."

Syrd sat silently at the table, listening to the small talk between Andra, Daëmon and Kiroyo. The way Andra talked to the old man was nothing short of insolence, but then she had behaved the same towards Dr Lascaux. That time in mental therapy Syrd had envied Andra's nerve. Those weeks of gruelling questioning and the interviews with Shenlyn and Cromer had nearly broken him. One slip would have exposed him, one wrong word. But he had not made a slip. And was he now to go through it again? That old man with the gold badge of rank? A social friend of Shenlyn? The continual probing questions and Andra watching? Is that why he was here? Because they had discovered Alexen and Buven and suspected him? Because he had not deceived Shenlyn and Cromer? Or because he had not deceived Andra? He should have had Andra removed before. She was dangerous.

Syrd did not understand that there was a close friendship between Andra and Kiroyo. He did not even know that friendship could exist between one so young and one so old, one so important as Kiroyo and one so unimportant as Andra. He did not know why Kiroyo had come and it made him wary.

Kiroyo emptied his plate, leaned back in his chair and stretched out his legs.

"Your cooking, Daëmon, is excellent," Kiroyo said.

"Compared with Andra's it certainly is," Daëmon agreed modestly.

"And which one of you is the artist?" Kiroyo asked as he surveyed the bright patterns on the walls.

Syrd eyed them: bright geometrical patterns, similar to thousands of others on the walls of thousands of other apartments throughout the city. They were the accepted form of art. And underneath them were Andra's paintings she dared not expose, paintings she should not have made. Andra's paintings were a deviation from conformity which Shenlyn, if he knew, would not tolerate.

"I designed them," Syrd said.

A sudden plan formed in his mind. He hesitated. Could he do that to Andra? Could he show Kiroyo what Andra was? Expose her rebellious nature? Have her sent for therapy or rehabilitation? Could he let them destroy Andra's mind? He was here to serve Grovinski so he had to. The ship would land within the month. He unclipped one of the designs and gave it to Kiroyo.

"You may have it if you like. I can do another."

Kiroyo did not take it from him. His eyes were riveted to the wall behind. Syrd felt a moment's unease. Kiroyo's eyes were as dark as Andra's.

Andra showed no apparent alarm that Syrd had

shown Kiroyo her painting. She looked almost smug. Kiroyo swung his chair round to face her.

"Did you paint that, Andra?"

"Yes, Papa Kiroyo, I painted it."

"What is it?"

"Don't you know?"

"I want you to tell me, Andra."

She smiled at the wall as if she did not see it. Slowly she went round the room taking down every one of Syrd's frescoes and exposing her own. Syrd had never seen them all together. They changed the room, making it look something like the gardens and yet nothing like them. It was a tangle of strange plants and creatures from another world.

Her voice spoke to them, rising and falling like the swell of water in the sea gardens Syrd had visited once many years ago.

"This is a rowan tree. They called it the tree of the mountains. These are maples in the autumn. This is a horse racing with the wind and clouds. These are birds, wild geese, flying northwards. This is a whippoorwill and reeds by a river. Here is the moon and an owl. Here is a lake with the sunset on it and there are pine trees on the hill. They are wild things, growing things, living things. Living, Kiroyo, living free in the sun."

Syrd was watching Kiroyo. The old man was not angry. He was not outraged. He sat there and nodded his head.

"Andra," Kiroyo said, "how did you know?"

"How did I know what, Papa Kiroyo?"

"How did you know how to paint them? How did you know their shapes and their colours? The things you have painted are true likenesses, but I have not shown you the books with pictures."

"I saw them," she said simply, "so long ago it's like remembering a dream, going back through time to when these things were real. I never knew what they were until I came to work with you. I used to see them in my mind and I didn't know what they were. I paint them as I saw them. I can only paint them. I can't bring them back."

"She tells us of them," Daëmon said, "of the books and the world as it used to be. We watch her when she paints. It is like hearing about a dream and then seeing it. It's not real."

"But they were real," Kiroyo said. "All these things were real. Andra, you astound me. It has to be your imagination that has created these things, and yet they are so lifelike I can almost believe you really *have* seen them."

"She has," Syrd said quietly. "Do you know about Andra, Professor? That little bit of brain Dr Lascaux put in her head, do you know where it came from? Do you know who shares your head, Andra?"

Andra scowled at him.

"Dr Lascaux told me his name was Richard Carson. I know he's here. I know it's he who puts these things in my mind because they weren't there before. Kiroyo knows too. I told him."

"But you don't know everything," Syrd said. "Dr Lascaux was worried about you. The way you reacted sometimes. When he knew we were to share the same apartment he asked me to watch you. He thought maybe you would need further treatment. And you do, don't you? Richard Carson died in 1987."

Kiroyo sat up straight.

"Yes, Professor. Richard Carson died in 1987. Those things on the wall are the things he saw."

There was a heavy silence, then a gurgle of laughter. Andra pushed back her cap and laughed.

"I wish you'd told me before, Syrd. I couldn't think how he knew so much. I'm glad I know. And this is supposed to be a party. Papa Kiroyo has come to hear you sing. So sing for us, Syrd."

Syrd followed her to the small room where she slept. Andra didn't care, she just didn't care. She knew Kiroyo wouldn't report her to Shenlyn. She'd cast a spell over him. She wouldn't be reported or rehabilitated and Syrd knew he was glad. He'd tried and failed. Grovinski wasn't important right now. Only Andra was and she'd probably hate him for what he had tried to do.

He watched her as she took the guitar from its case. A lock of hair had escaped from her cap. He took it in his hand. It was warm and smooth and long. He pulled the cap from her head and her hair fell around her shoulders, black as the knobs on the computer. She was a strange and beautiful girl.

"I'm sorry," Syrd said softly. "I just didn't think. I forgot your painting was underneath when I gave him that one."

She dropped the guitar on the bed, stared at him and piled her hair back in her cap. Then she smiled.

"It doesn't matter. That's why I brought him here. I wanted him to see them. I thought maybe he'd tell me why I painted them. But you did that. Why didn't you tell me before about Richard Carson?"

"Dr Lascaux thought it better that you shouldn't know."

"So now I do. And you think I'm mad and need treatment."

"Not mad," Syrd said. He took up the guitar and played a gentle note. "Not mad. Worse than mad. Growing your hair long. If someone sees that: phut! Cromer will have you expired. I think I shall tell Kiroyo."

Andra laughed.

"Papa Kiroyo already knows. And when you play for him he will also know that someone has stolen a guitar from his sacred museum. He might be very angry and report *you*."

Syrd strummed a mellow chord.

In less than a month he would do what he had come to do and then Grovinski would mean nothing at all. It wouldn't matter then what Andra said or did. He wouldn't need to pretend to be on her side. He could really join her.

11

She was a bright dot on the radar screen.

"With another two-second burst we could bring her down tonight," Fenner remarked.

"And will you?" Daëmon asked.

"I think so. Can you stand the pace? It will mean four hours of tension."

"I slept this afternoon. I'm not tired now."

"Good. Your senses need to be sharp. I can leave her or bring her down. I think I shall give you the choice."

"But you are in control, Fenner. I said I'm not tired. Bring her down and I will co-operate. I shan't let you down."

Fenner regarded the young man he worked so closely with: Daëmon, leader of the youth centre, brilliant with radar and only eighteen years old. Fenner knew that soon this fair-haired youth would replace him as head of space control room. The knowledge did not make him bitter but heightened the regard he had for his successor. If Daëmon was ready to bring the ship down then he had no need to worry. Daëmon would obey his smallest instruction instantly.

Fenner nodded his head. Four hours was not so very long to be on their toes. He had worked for more than forty hours before without sleep.

"Two-second burst on numbers fifteen and sixteen."

Daëmon flicked on the switches, watched the time pass on the chronometer and flicked off.

A voice said:

"Height 3,000. Speed 983."

Daëmon said:

"She's coming in fast."

Fenner nodded.

"And we have all the time in the world to slow her down. Get Cromer on the phone."

Daëmon buzzed security. The conversation was brief.

"Cromer is on his way here," he informed Fenner. "He sounded a little put out."

Fenner glanced at the huge room, at the row of computers along the one wall and the men in yellow clothes who worked there. There was the great television screen which showed the stars in the sky above them and somewhere among the stars was the ship they were bringing home. Fenner could not pick her out and the fact that Cromer might be annoyed was no concern of his.

"Why don't you snatch a break?" the older man suggested. "I'll join you as soon as I've seen Cromer. There's nothing we can do here until she enters the stratosphere."

Daëmon nodded his head and left the radar screen. She was still just a steady dot, she wouldn't change much for another couple of hours. But he had not been able to meet Andra at the youth centre tonight. He wondered if Andra would be angry, then dismissed her from his mind to slap Syrd on the back.

"Fenner is landing her tonight," Daëmon said. "Are you staying for the fun?"

Syrd stiffened.

"Tonight? I thought it was tomorrow morning?"

"It was. He's increased her speed."

Syrd kept his eye on the computer. He hadn't wanted to be here for this.

"Where is she now?"

"A little under 3,000."

At 1,000 the contact would be cut. Syrd knew that. He had taken the cathode electron away yesterday, when he had done a final routine check on the computer. He had done what they had sent him to do. The ship would crash, but he hadn't planned to be there when it happened.

"Which idiot spilt his drink inside the works? The chronometer on this computer has gone completely haywire. It's going to take me all night to fix it."

"Computer operator three: that'll be Hanman. He is a bit absent-minded. Come and have a drink with me, Syrd, or can't you spare the time?"

Syrd snapped shut his bag of tools.

"I may as well. I shall have to go to the store and fetch a new 3.2 coil. So she's coming down, then? What time is Shenlyn due to arrive?"

"If I know Fenner," Daëmon said, "he'll conveniently forget to inform Shenlyn at all."

Cromer said:

"They tell me you were asking for me."

"Oh yes," Fenner confirmed without looking round. "We're bringing the ship down tonight. Would you be good enough to ensure that all personnel in the landing area are standing by. Estimated touch-down: 0323 hours."

Cromer looked at Fenner sharply.

"I was informed this morning that she would not be down until 1100 hours tomorrow."

"Today," Fenner corrected. "It's past midnight."

"You should have consulted me, Fenner. Has Shenlyn been notified?"

"He has not."

"You wish me to do so?"

Cromer's purple uniform was harshly glaring in the strong light.

"No, thank you. I manage better without Shenlyn breathing down my neck. We'll give him a surprise in the morning, eh, Cromer?"

Cromer clicked his heels and strode away. He had no sense of humour.

Fenner and Daëmon were back in the control room three minutes before 0230 hours. And at 0255 hours Syrd was still working on computer three. The extreme tension which was building up inside him made his fingers fumble.

Fenner looked round and remarked:

106

"Still at it, Syrd?"

Syrd nodded.

"I thought I'd better stick around just in case I'm needed."

"Good heavens," Fenner replied. "I hope you're not."

Good heavens, Syrd thought. I wish it was tomorrow morning and everything was all over. Damn the man who spilt his drink. I didn't want to be here to see this.

"How far away is she now?"

Daëmon's voice was strained:

"She will be entering the stratosphere in seventy-nine seconds."

The room was electric with tension. The ship was coming in fast. Every man was keyed to breaking point, waiting for the orders to slow her down. Fenner's eyes were glued to the clock. Her height was 1,097 and there were twenty-two seconds left.

His hand was poised and his voice was calm.

"Ten seconds on five, twelve seconds on one. Number four all she's got . . . Now!"

The men depressed the switches, each obeying his separate command. Daëmon watched the radar screen.

"Now!" Fenner shouted again. "Correction: thirteen seconds on five. Now!"

"Five not answering."

"Four not answering."

"One not answering."

Twenty seconds had gone by.

"Speed 1,097, height 983."

Fenner's face was drained of all colour.

"Number two, number three, number seven: all they've got. Slow her down. Try number eight."

"Speed 1,683. Height 928."

"If we turned her now maybe we could use the dorsal motors. They fired to give her the boost in speed."

Fenner took up Daëmon's suggestion.

"Turn: 180 degrees."

Silence.

"Is she answering?"

"Half turn 90 degrees completed. 95, 105 . . . 175, 180. Turn complete."

"Dorsal motors: 25-second burst all numbers."

"She's not answering, sir."

"She's getting hot," Daëmon remarked.

"And she'll get hotter if she hits the air at that speed. Syrd! Syrd! Come here quick! You've got sixty seconds to find out what's wrong with that computer."

Syrd fought down his panic.

"There's nothing wrong with it. I checked it a few weeks ago on Cromer's instructions and again yesterday."

"There must be something wrong with it. Find the fault, boy. Contact is broken with the motors. Come on, lad. Find it before it's too late."

Syrd slipped the back off the machine and hoped Fenner wouldn't notice he was shaking.

"Speed 3,726. Height 643."

Fenner thumped the computer.

"Anything?"

"Nothing," Syrd lied. The cathode electron control was missing. It lay in the bottom of his pocket like a lump of lead.

"Orbit her," Daëmon said.

"We could lose her. She'll shoot back."

"Not if we're careful. We'll lose her anyway. She'll burn up if she continues at that rate."

"OK," muttered Fenner. "I'm ready. You call."

"Twenty-five degrees now."

"She's coming. Twenty-five complete."

"Thirty-five degrees now."

"Thirty-five complete."

"Hold it. OK. Hold it. Five degrees now. Another five now.

"Height 409. Speed steady."

"She's going too fast to hold an orbit."

"I know. Eleven degrees now. That's why I'm calling and calling. *We'll* have to keep her in orbit. She'll come nearer each round but she'll also slow a little. 3.4 degrees now. Maybe with a bit of luck . . ."

Fenner's hands were wet with sweat. It hung on his forehead in bright beads and trickled down his face.

"Daëmon, she's too damn fast. You know she is."

"Nine degrees now."

"Height 227. Speed 2,545."

"You see: she has slowed slightly."

"But not enough. Not enough."

"Seven degrees now. Now thirteen."

"Daëmon, we can't bring her in at this speed."

"And what else can we do with no motors? Radio contact yet?"

"No radio contact."

Fenner bit his lip.

"Is it us or the ship? Is it the computer, Syrd?"

"There is nothing wrong with this computer unless it's a microscopic fault which might take days to find. How can it be the computer? It was thoroughly checked. I told you it was."

"Height 190. Speed 2,373."

"Five degrees. Two degrees. Three degrees."

"Daëmon, be careful. One degree out and she'll shoot back."

"I *am* being careful. 4.5 degrees."

"Fins out, parachute out," Fenner snapped.

"The parachute has ignited," came the reply. "Fins in position."

"Height 123. Speed 1,635."

"Nine degrees. Seven degrees."

"Height 63. Speed 745. She's feeling the effect of the fins, sir."

"Switch on the homing beam," Daëmon instructed. "She's too low to take round again."

Fenner groaned.

"We've had it. She's coming and she's too fast. We've had it."

"I know," the young man said. "You don't have to tell me. Where is she?"

"Mid-Atlantic. Height 23. Speed 233."

"Ditch her in the sea."

"Oh, Fenner. Don't suggest mad things. She's on the homing beam. We can't turn her now. We've just got to sit back and wait for the bang."

"Height 19. Speed 199."

"Don't bother," Daëmon said heavily. "Her speed and position don't matter. She'll land bang on her bottom in the middle of the landing pit."

Syrd slipped the cathode electron back into the computer. He had done what he had been sent here to do. The ship would crash. All they had told him about Uralian supremacy didn't mean a thing. He wished he was dead.

He snapped on the back of the computer.

"There's nothing wrong with it," he repeated.

Fenner leant heavily against the switchboard. All she needed was a turn of ninety degrees, give the dorsal motors all they'd got and she'd make a perfect landing. He depressed the switches.

"Hell's bells!" shrieked Daëmon. "What are you doing? She's fired. She's got out of the beam. Fenner, where's that ship?"

Fenner didn't know. He hung on to the control for dear life and knew she was turning. Fifty degrees, sixty degrees, all rockets firing. Ten seconds, fifteen seconds. He sank down on to the chair.

They located her. She had landed at a speed of

sixty miles an hour. Belly-dived into the side of a hill. She had been away for almost a hundred years and she had almost made it home. She was a wreck, only twenty miles away from the landing pit. The tireless computers whirred on.

"You tried, Fenner," Daëmon said. "You tried but it was too late. She went down like a bomb."

Fenner stared at the boy as though he hardly knew him. Half-an-hour had drained him of everything. He had no spirit left. He ran his fingers through his hair. He would not be rejuvenated again. He was tired.

Fenner said:

"Who's going to tell Shenlyn?"

Syrd slipped away.

SHENLYN

12

Shenlyn was irritated. He had overslept and someone had woken him in the middle of a dream. He
could have murdered that stony-faced domestic
who had told him. If Fenner had been around he
would have murdered him too. He had crawled
out of bed with eyes still heavy from interrupted
sleep and raged at them all. Then they had told
him Renson had gone on and taken his car. There
was none other available and they were waiting
for him at the site. He, Shenlyn, had to walk.

The Director of Sub-city One strode through
the streets looking to neither right nor left. He
did not acknowledge the salutes of the people, nor
smile at their awe that Shenlyn, the great Director,
should pass among them. His fair hair straggled
over his eyes and his face was as grim as the grey
road that led to the factories and the laboratories.
Shenlyn elbowed his way through the mass of
people, cursing silently when they did not see him
coming and make a way for him, cursing because
he could not walk faster, and cursing Cromer
because he had not told him personally. His cloak
was heavy and wrapped round his legs, which
impeded his progress. He was hot and sweating
and his right boot had developed a squeak. This
irritated Shenlyn even more.

As he walked through the outskirts of the city the streets became deserted. From behind closed doors came the hum of voices and the whirr of machinery. He quickened his pace. They were waiting for him. The security men who followed him had to trot to keep up. He heard their feet pattering behind him and their noisy breathing as the road led them upwards. The patter patter of their footsteps got on his nerves and so did the squeak of his boot. What a confounded thing to happen!

One hundred years that ship had been roaming round the stars. One hundred years and the mechanism had been faultless. One hundred years to boost their hopes and the damn thing had crashed twenty miles from the landing pit. Why? What had gone wrong? Metal fatigue? A fault in the automatic steering device? A fault in the computer? Or a fault in the ship? Shenlyn didn't know, but it was imperative they should find out. Damn Renson! He might have waited. Shenlyn disliked people who were more efficient than himself. Renson had rounded up the salvage team whilst he, Shenlyn, had been asleep in bed. Fenner had landed the ship whilst he, Shenlyn, had been in bed. Cromer had known and not one of them had woken him up. One hundred bloody years and he hadn't been there to see the end. Why had it happened? Why hadn't he been told? Damn it, why?

He reached the escalator. It went up so slowly.

He couldn't see the top. He started to walk up, the stairs moving with him and the watchdogs moving behind him. Dog? What did that word mean? Nothing! Absolutely nothing! It was just an expression that had survived from prehistoric times. He should have gone up in the lift, it would have been quicker, but the lift was reserved for vehicles only and Shenlyn always obeyed his own rules.

The escalator vomited Shenlyn on to the concrete floor of the upper landing. He strode to the door and pressed the button. It whined open and he strode into a vast cavern, so vast that it was impossible to see the far walls or the roof. The cold air bit into his teeth. It would be freezing outside. He thrust his gloved hands deep into the pockets of his cloak. Somewhere at the other end of the cavern he could hear the noise of metal clanking. It was very faint and far away, but it told Shenlyn that the men were working on the ships. He was too far away to see them and right now he was not concerned with the fleet of ships still under construction. His limited sight at last showed him the bus and the convoy of freight wagons. He lengthened his stride.

Shenlyn swung himself aboard the bus and nodded to the driver. The vehicle purred away and he heard the roar of the wagons as they prepared to follow. The door of the bus closed behind him with a muffled thud and he dropped thankfully into the vacant seat beside Renson. He nodded curtly to his deputy and retired into brooding silence, his chin sunk deep into the collar of his cloak.

The bus ate its way up the steep gradient of the tunnel. The way was unlit and the headlights stabbed the darkness with bars of yellow light. The road to the surface was hardly ever used and it was pitted and uneven, causing the bus to shudder and jolt until it sighed to a halt. The driver left his seat to go outside and open the doors. Shenlyn frowned. The doors should be automated. This part of the city was falling behind the times. It was only a small delay, a small time taken to walk outside and press a button, but any delay immediately irritated the Director of Sub-city One.

The great doors opened with a hiss and the brilliant daylight rushed in. The bus moved forward, out of its confines underground, up on to the barren surface of the earth. The light surrounded them and Shenlyn closed his eyes against the glare. It was too harsh a light, his eyes were unused to it. He took a pair of dark glasses from the compartment below the seat. Then he began to feel the cold. It crept through the windows and through his cloak, making his skin prickle with gooseflesh. It might be summer and the sun might be shining, but it was still cold. He watched his breath curl whitely into the air and mingle with the breath of Renson until the heaters boosted the temperature to a more congenial level and he could no longer see it. The windows steamed over and Shenlyn knew it would take this slow cumbersome vehicle over an hour to travel the thirty miles across the roadless terrain.

It did not take many minutes for Shenlyn to become bored. He was not used to sitting still, idling time away. He could not see the world outside through the misted windows. He did not want to see it. He had seen it before and it was no novelty to him. It was bleak and hostile and he had no liking for it. His eyes roamed restlessly over the assortment of people around him.

He had left his bodyguard back at the city. Security men would not be needed on this trip. There was the driver. Shenlyn didn't know him. He was just a driver, IQ probably below 100. Behind him were Fenner and his young assistant. Shenlyn thought Fenner didn't look too happy. He tried to remember how many years he had left to live before his next injection. Not many, and after this catastrophe he would not be rejuvenated again. He stared at the fair curls of Fenner's assistant. He had been informed he was unusually brilliant and he was a mere eighteen years of age. His name was Daëmon. He was popular among the young people, they had made him leader at the youth centre. Probably it would be Daëmon who took Fenner's place. Then Shenlyn hesitated over such a decision. No, Daëmon would not become head of space control, he was too young. He was young enough and efficient

119

enough to qualify for the trip to 801. Captain the mother ship maybe? Shenlyn nodded to himself. He had found the leader for the city they would build on that other planet thirty years away from them.

He left Daëmon, passed over the dull green uniform of the six mechanics, over the four electricians who wore navy-blue. He didn't know them. Yes he did! He knew one, the singer who had come to them from Uralia. He had made a name for himself, had that young man. Shenlyn had not been too happy when Lascaux and Cromer advised him to let the boy live without rehabilitation, but he was proving his worth. He was a brilliant electrician. Shenlyn tried to remember the words of the song;

Omyara: I run through whirling patterns
For something that my mind will not define
Through the curving passages of time.
And when I found you, Omyara, you were
    gone.

Not right, not right, but he had the tune. Syrd was clever, very clever. The young ones worshipped him. He, too, would go to 801.

There were two men for data processing, two technicians, two radiologists and the drivers of the freight wagons to do the actual body salvage work. Immediately in front of himself and Renson sat Kiroyo. Shenlyn frowned. He was not surprised to see Kiroyo here, he usually came when there was a trip to the surface, but why bring the girl? Shenlyn would have argued but he had been asleep and Renson had not had the imagination to argue. This was no place for a girl, but he supposed they would both potter among the ruins and not bother him. He frowned at the back of her head and felt irritated again. He watched her wipe the condensation from the window and heard her laugh. Shenlyn was in no mood for laughter. Her familiarity with Kiroyo was apparent in the way she talked to him, almost ceaselessly chattering. How insolent she was! She should not speak to him unless he asked her to do so. Shenlyn leant forward to catch her words. Hell! She was talking in ancient English.

He found himself watching the girl from the archives: her fine chiselled profile gazed intently from the window at the sky. She had not seen it before. Watching her expression and her movements, listening to the rise and fall of her voice became a kind of occupation to him. Her voice had a musical quality, a lilt which made it pleasant to the ear. She wore a silver cap and a strand of hair had escaped: short and black. That was what made Shenlyn remember: this girl was Dr Lascaux's pride and joy, the girl with the brain graft which had been so successful it had turned her hair from fair to black. Shenlyn remembered how he had laughed when Lascaux had told him, but really it wasn't funny. Black hair must be a constant source of discontent for the girl. So they had sent her to assist Kiroyo. Of course: Kiroyo and Renson had been talking about her a few weeks ago.

Shenlyn scowled at the back of her head.

She was the girl who had reportedly said: "Pot to Shenlyn."

He hoped he would not have occasion to speak to her.

13

They had been working hard all day. The sun had swung across the sky from east to west. Much of the ship had been loaded on to the wagons. They would be finished by noon tomorrow. Over the more delicate pieces of mechanism the electricians, technicians and mechanics still worked, but they would not work for much longer, the light was beginning to fail. The small far-away sun hung suspended for a while over the rim of the mountains under which the Sub-city was built. Shenlyn watched it as it began to disappear slowly, a pale yellow ball of glowing light without the faintest trace of warmth, and the shadows of the mountains crept nearer to him. The twilight was becoming gloomy and the cross on the hill stood starkly black. They had buried the crew there all in one grave.

Shenlyn, too, had worked with the rest of them, abandoning his position and heaving pieces of rocket on to the wagon with his massive strength. Now his limbs were aching. They were objecting to work after so many years of disuse. He sat on a packing case sipping the hot sweet drink and frowning round on his subordinates who were now dark silhouettes against the lighted tents. It had been more than fifty years since he last slept in the open.

The bitter wind swept over the desolate plain. There were no trees to temper its wrath and the sun of the summer had not warmed it. It howled mournfully around the tents, drying their lips and their faces until the skin split and bled. When the sun had gone a strange luminous glow hung above the mountains, which stretched their craggy peaks towards it. The snow on their summits shone pink. Shenlyn's hands were numb with the cold and the warmth of the cup caused him pain. He hoped he would not be sleeping in the open again for another fifty years. His spirit of adventure had been evaporated by the cold.

They paused quite close to him, the girl and Kiroyo. Shenlyn sank against the shadow of his unlit tent. He had no wish to converse with either of them. The world of books which Kiroyo knew so well was out of place on this cold empty surface. Shenlyn did not want to know about how things used to be.

"It's gone, Kiroyo," Andra said.

Shenlyn gripped the cup tighter. That girl! She had no respect. Just "Kiroyo" she had called him. He should be "Professor Kiroyo" to her.

"It always does, my dear, at the end of the day."

"Tomorrow we shall return underground and I shall never see it again. The sky is pretty but it is not red, and orange, and yellow, flaming with hot

124

colours of the sun. It is a cool pale pink behind the mountains. The mountains have a lovely name, Kiroyo, don't you think so?"

"Spanish," Kiroyo murmured.

Andra laughed.

"Spanish guitars, twinkling stars, roses, moon, tune and June. All those romantic words have no meaning now. It makes me sad. It makes me sad that there will be no moon and tomorrow no sun. See, the clouds pile up behind us and in the morning they will cover the sun."

"Are you regretting you came, Andra?"

"A little, maybe. I thought I would see it as it used to be. I was thinking it would be green and it's grey. Look at it, Kiroyo, look at it. Once there were trees here and now there are rocks. There is sand where flowers used to grow and heaps of rubble where cities used to be. Look at it: not one living thing on the whole of its great barren surface. This is what they made of something beautiful; this great ugly grey desert, and I have to suffer for what they did."

She shivered.

"How cold is the wind. It bites through my flesh and reaches the bone. My blood turns to ice. The clouds cover the moon and the sun is gone and thirty men lie beneath the earth's frozen surface in one communal grave. Tomorrow I'll be buried as well, deep down under the mountains in Sub-city One."

Kiroyo shuffled his feet uneasily. He hoped

Andra was not about to voice an attack on Administration. He saw the flush on her cheeks and his unease increased. Shenlyn was somewhere around. Kiroyo had been afraid to tell Andra Shenlyn was with them, he had been afraid she might take the opportunity to tell Shenlyn exactly what she thought of his Administration. Kiroyo had wisely held his tongue and prayed to the strange person they had worshipped long ago: "God make her hold her tongue too."

She was staring at the outline of the mountains.

"How many more centuries do we have to be cooped up under the ground like scuttling termites?" Andra asked. "It's all wrong. Not so much *where* we live but *how* we live. We're like empty shells, not people. Even our thoughts are moulded by EDCO. We can't feel anything because we've forgotten how. Do you know what I mean? There's nothing individual any more. We work because we have to work not because we want to. And we do the particular work we're assigned to because we can't do any other kind of work even if we want to. We're not people any more, we're just things. We're born, and taught, and work, and live, and then we die. There's no freedom, no emotions, no sensation, no expression, and it's wrong. It's wrong, Kiroyo. I should like to put Shenlyn in a bag and shake him."

Shenlyn put down his mug and quelled his anger. He rose to join them and honoured Kiroyo with a curt nod. The girl glanced at him indifferently.

Shenlyn said:

"The lady is displeased with us?"

Andra did not bother to reply. Her brown eyes were far away and brooding.

"The hour is late," Shenlyn said. "It grows cold beyond endurance. Your tent is there by the far wagon. Go to bed, child, and sleep away your ill-humour."

Kiroyo closed his eyes.

"God make her do what she is told."

Syrd and Daëmon came from their tent. She ran towards them.

"Syrd, Daëmon, did you bring your vinets?"

Shenlyn smiled grimly at Kiroyo.

"I now understand your reluctance when I bade you take an assistant."

The old man looked puzzled.

"She is a violent young lady. Not one of EDCO's better products. You find her hard to handle?"

Kiroyo took off his spectacles. The sun had made his eyes ache and Shenlyn was waiting for an answer. Did he find Andra hard to handle?

"She is impossible to handle," Kiroyo murmured. "Even *you* could not handle her, Shenlyn, and yet I think she is the most entrancing person it has been my pleasure to meet."

Old man, Shenlyn thought, your brain has become addled. The girl has cast a spell over you.

127

"You are prepared to defend her? A little nonentity? A rebellious minx who questions our right to exist? Why did you bring her, Kiroyo? This is no place for a girl. She should have stayed in the archives and fed the computer."

"I bring her because she asks to come."

"That is not a reason."

"I bring her because she wishes to see the sun."

"Nor is that a reason. It should not be what she wants to do but what she ought to do."

"Should it?" Kiroyo murmured. "A little of what we want should not be amiss."

Shenlyn ignored this.

"So she would like to put me in a bag and shake me? I did not hear you reprimand her for her manner of speech."

Kiroyo patted Shenlyn's arm.

"She is free to speak what she will to me, my friend. I am older than you. I have lived long enough to know that the thoughts of individuals are not identical, nor are the ideas of one man entirely right, and that includes you, Sir Director. If Andra thinks it would be good to put you in a bag and shake you why should she not say so, eh? Maybe Kiroyo will help her."

Shenlyn almost laughed. He was defeated and yet he could laugh. "What, Kiroyo, would you defy me to save a girl from my displeasure? She makes you become a senile old man and she makes the eyes of Syrd and Daëmon glow with pleasure when she calls their names.

"What name did you call her?" Shenlyn asked.

"Andra," Kiroyo said.

"Andra," repeated Shenlyn. "I will remember the lady Andra if ever we are unfortunate enough to meet again."

14

Next morning it began to snow, small flakes whirled by the wind to slap their faces with an icy hand. And the wind whined continually like an irritated child and played with the snow, throwing it, catching it, scooping it from the ground in twirling eddies of white coldness. The snow and the wind were all around them and their work became slower and more difficult. Hands were numb, faces were frozen and tempers torn to shreds.

It was early when the girl rushed into camp. The ground was hardly smeared with white and her cries of excitement called everyone from their work. The wind had brought a pink flush to her cheeks which made her almost pretty, but Shenlyn only frowned at the distraction she was causing.

"Look!" she cried. "Look! It's not dead, not quite."

The men gathered round her. In her open palm she displayed a green plant with a white starry flower.

"See!" she said. "Something lives. Something has found a way to exist, not beneath the surface like we do, but up here in the wind and the sun."

"What is it?" Syrd asked her.

"Moss. Kiroyo is collecting other samples for the botanists to examine. It's not a real flower, just the spore head, but it's pretty, don't you think?"

Shenlyn thrust another fragment of the ship on to the wagon and turned to stare at the girl. Her face was flushed, but that was normal after physical exertion, and her cloak had slipped from her shoulders exposing the skin of her neck. Shenlyn frowned. There was something wrong with her. A lock of hair had escaped from her cap and he could see the snow hanging like stars on its blackness. Her hair was long, almost to her waist.

Shenlyn felt his anger mounting. The moss did not matter. How dare this girl grow her hair long! It was barbaric and uncivilised. It was rebellion against society. No one had long hair. With a few strides he reached her and tore the cap from her head. Her hair fell around her in black waves, warm as the feathers of extinct birds and whirling in the wind like a witch's cape.

Shenlyn stared round at the ring of silent faces. Most of them showed bemused surprise, but the face of the young electrician was white, so too was the face of Daëmon who was so much in Shenlyn's favour. He looked back at the girl. She stared at the whitely gleaming ground. Well might she hang her head in shame, but no, she was not ashamed. She lifted her head and the laughter rippled from her lips to be snatched away by the wind. Her dark eyes sparkled with some devilment which had escaped from her inner soul.

Daëmon touched her arm.

"Andra, don't laugh."

She flung back her dancing hair and laughed again.

"Don't you like my hair, Daëmon?"

Daëmon bit his lips. He could see the wrath on Shenlyn's face. How could Andra stand there and laugh when the Director of Sub-city One was angry with her? He wanted to warn her but he dared not. Didn't the little idiot realise who Shenlyn was?

Shenlyn himself was grim. Never before had he been laughed at by a mere commoner. This girl must be taught humility. She must be taught to obey the rules of the city, *his* city. She needed mental therapy immediately.

"Get back to your work," Shenlyn ordered the men.

They departed obediently. The girl, too, turned to go.

Shenlyn grasped her hair.

"Not you, lady. You and I need to understand each other a little better."

He was hurting her. He saw the pain flicker in her eyes.

"What is this?" asked Shenlyn.

"You know damn well what it is. It's hair. My hair. Let go of it, please, you're hurting me."

He thrust its black warmth into her face.

132

"It disgusts me," Shenlyn said.

Her head lifted proudly.

"Why should I care what you think? I am not destined to live with you. I like it long and I shall keep it long and if you don't like it you know what you can do."

Shenlyn fought to keep his anger under control. Never had he been spoken to like this before. How dare this girl stand there and defy him!

"Do you know who I am?" he snapped.

She eyed him up and down, scowling in dislike of what she saw. The pale blue uniform of Administration did not frighten her but merely increased her resentment.

"I've not the slightest idea who you are. I assume you are one of Shenlyn's inferiors."

The man's fists clenched at his side. She was making him very angry. Andra shrugged her shoulders and turned to go. Administration! She had no patience with them. Do this, don't do that, think this, don't think that: hell, it was worse than the ten commandments they obeyed in the old days. At least one could break the ten commandments if one did not possess a troublesome conscience. Here they could do nothing unless Administration approved. But one day, if she had her way, things were going to change.

She flicked back her hair.

"Kiroyo is waiting for me," she said over her shoulder. "Goodbye, sir."

Shenlyn felt something snap inside him. He gripped her shoulders and swung her round.

"When we return to the city, girl, you will go immediately to the mental therapy unit. Tell Dr Lascaux I sent you. You will undergo two months of treatment, and after that I will personally consult Dr Lascaux about your fitness to return to work."

Her lips moved silently. He wondered if she would cry. He had never seen tears but he believed they were a symptom of mental depression. But no, her brown eyes stared with annoyance and her lips curled scornfully.

"I feel sorry for you," she remarked. "I feel sorry for your poor narrow mind and your overwhelming sense of self-importance. I don't take orders from you, only from Kiroyo."

She tried to shake herself from his grasp.

"Lady, your insolence has gone too far and your ignorance astounds me. You will go for mental therapy as I instructed."

Andra and Shenlyn were angry. Syrd and Daëmon could hear their raised voices and looked at each other in alarm. Syrd picked up a metal bar and regarded Shenlyn thoughtfully, but the Director was not actually hurting Andra.

"Put it down," Daëmon said. "You can't attack Shenlyn. Andra is being completely idiotic. What does she think she's doing talking to Shenlyn like that? She must know she'll only make trouble for herself."

"Andra," said Syrd, "probably doesn't know she's talking to Shenlyn. I don't think she's ever seen him."

"Phew!" muttered Daëmon. "So she doesn't know. By the look of it she is about to be enlightened."

"You know something?" Syrd asked, swinging the metal bar.

"What?"

"It's funny. Look at their faces. I shall laugh."

Daëmon saw what he meant.

Andra heard the faint trickle of Syrd's laughter and inwardly seethed. Her hair was getting in her eyes and the piece of moss was being crushed. She stamped her foot.

"Let me go! Let me go at once! Who are you to give me orders? You have no badge of rank. You're just a nobody from Administration who has grown too big for his boots. I shall report you to Professor Kiroyo."

He released her.

"I do not need a badge of rank. My name is Shenlyn and you, lady, are not fit to exist. I am being lenient with you. You should be rehabilitated. Now go! Cover your filthy tresses so that they do not pollute the eyes of better men."

Andra's eyes flashed, then she turned on her heel and walked quickly away. She walked between the men, ignoring their questions and flinging an angry remark at Syrd and Daëmon who were still laughing. The wind blew her hair round her face and her silver cloak billowed out behind her. Shenlyn watched her, still holding her cap, and felt a gleam of admiration. She had an incredible nerve.

So she had disobeyed and grown her hair long. It had slipped through his fingers like synthetic fur. Had he been right to punish her? Her small act of rebellion could not disturb the conformity of the city, but even a small rebellion must be squashed before it began and developed into something more. She was a friend of the singer and a friend of the youth leader and he could not afford to cosset trouble among the young people. Yes, he had been right to punish her.

Kiroyo was standing behind Shenlyn.

"So you found out?" the old man murmured. "I said she was a naughty girl."

Shenlyn rounded on him.

"You knew," he roared. "You knew and you did nothing about it? Be careful, Kiroyo. I think you are getting too old."

Kiroyo grinned. Probably he knew Shenlyn better than anyone. This big bear of a man with his curved nose and frowning brows did not frighten Kiroyo. Kiroyo never doubted his right to exist. He was unique and indispensable and no one could take his place. Only Andra, and Andra was in trouble.

He patted Shenlyn's arm.

"She has made you angry, my friend? How often does she make me angry? Many, many times. She laughs at me too, but I find it easier to laugh with her than go against her. I warn you, Shenlyn, if you fight Andra you will lose. She always wins in the end."

Shenlyn banged his fist in his palm.

"Kiroyo, you poor addled old man, I shall send you another assistant. That young lady must be put to something more routine."

Kiroyo glanced up at Shenlyn. So Andra had begun a fight with him. It was a regrettable thing to have happened. But Shenlyn could not take Andra away so he, Kiroyo, was obliged to take her side.

Kiroyo said:

"That would be most foolish, Shenlyn. You should reconsider, I think. Little Andra could be the stick in the hornet's nest. Put her among the bees and she will stir them to fury. You, my dear friend, might get sorely stung. She is far safer away in the archives with me. And if you wish to leave for 801 within the next eighteen months Andra *must* stay."

"What has 801 to do with that girl?"

"It has much to do with her. Without information from my archives you will not be able to survive on 801. You will not know how to live. If you take Andra away I shall refuse to feed the computer."

Shenlyn stared at Kiroyo.

"But that is blackmail."

"Yes, it is blackmail. I take it you have reconsidered, and my assistant will be returned to me?"

"It seems I have very little choice," Shenlyn said sourly. "But I have ordered the lady Andra to take a course of mental therapy. Must I reconsider that also?"

Kiroyo chuckled.

"For that, my friend, I am thankful. After what has passed between you two, Andra will be seething with fury. I feel relieved that it will be Dr Lascaux and not I who will receive the full blast of her temper. Now, Shenlyn, I have collected several samples of this little plant. It ought to go to the bio-lab immediately."

"We shall be leaving within three hours," Shenlyn informed him coldly.

He watched Kiroyo shuffle away. The girl had changed him from a mild old man into a conniving villain. A chit of a girl had undermined his own importance and scorned the very basis of their society. Shenlyn wanted to wring Andra's neck.

15

Everything was ready. The camp had been dismantled and the men climbed thankfully into the warmth of the vehicles. Shenlyn took a last look at the desolate whitening wind-swept world before he swung himself aboard. The heat swirled around his eyes and his tired limbs began to relax. The men talked together in lighthearted conversation. There was laughter as their cold bodies began to thaw and snow dripped from their mantles to form pools on the floor. Outside the wind still howled mournfully, but in here they could not feel it. Shenlyn nodded to the driver and sank thankfully into his seat.

Renson had a wide grin across his face.

"They have been telling me," he remarked, "that you had a slanging match with Kiroyo's little girl and came out the loser."

Shenlyn's reply was lost under the loud purr of the engine. The sad song of the wind could no longer be heard. Renson threw back his head and laughed at Shenlyn's discomfort. They were going home.

Kiroyo touched the Director's shoulder and whispered a brief word in his ear.

Shenlyn's relaxation was brief.

"Stop," he ordered the driver. "The girl isn't here."

The whine of the engine ceased and the whine of the wind took over again.

"Syrd," asked Kiroyo, "have you seen Andra?"

The young electrician was not laughing now. His eyes were troubled as he reached for his wet cloak. Daëmon too stood up and Kiroyo was agitated.

"Shall we search for her, sir?" Daëmon asked.

Shenlyn struggled to his feet.

"Stay here," he ordered. "I'll go. I don't believe in violence, Kiroyo, but that little wretch needs a smacked backside."

He left the warmth of the bus and faced the wind. The girl could not be far away. She must be cold for he still had her cap. He passed the remains of the camp almost invisible in the deepening snow. He drew his hands under his cloak and bent his head to the ground. The snow almost blinded him. He strode on. Where was the confounded girl? Probably over one hill in the ruins where they had found the plant.

For a moment the wind dropped and the snow eased and Shenlyn could look around him. He saw her standing at the foot of the hill, her hair whipping madly around her face. Shenlyn stiffened. She wasn't alone. There was someone standing on the top of the hill like a shadow against the skyline. Just for a moment he saw him, and then there was only Andra staring up the white hill above her.

"Andra!" Shenlyn shouted. "We are waiting for you."

She glanced over her shoulder and started running, not *to* him, but *away* from him. Shenlyn was in no mood to play games with her. He pounded after her through the whirling snow and his right palm itched. Up the hill and the wind took the air from his mouth before he could breathe. Then the sudden quietness where the ground was brown with sweet-smelling pine needles and the trees grew so thickly together that the snow could not penetrate their greenness.

Shenlyn blinked. The cold was distorting his sight. It formed strange pictures that danced before his eyes. He ran faster into the snow again, stumbling over the ruins of the buildings which the weather had eroded into part of the landscape. Upwards again towards the sky and his breath was rasping hotly through his teeth. He was very close behind her now. The snow flew from beneath her feet as she led Shenlyn upwards towards the great flying sky.

He put on a final spurt and clawed at her cloak to haul her backwards and grasp her firmly. The ground fell away beneath their feet to the river far below which churned angrily over the rocks foaming and grey. The rushing sound of its water echoed up from the face of the cliff and was caught by the wind and changed to music.

"I have run, I have run,
For so long I have run,
Through the curving passages of time.
And when I found you, Omyara, you were
    gone."

"You little fool," Shenlyn said angrily.
"Another two paces and you would have been
gone."

Her face was white as she started back down
the slope. Shenlyn followed her then paused to
look back. He sensed there was someone watching
him, but the grim grey skyline was empty save for
falling snow.

DAËMON

16

Daëmon paced the floor of the empty youth centre scowling at his boots, his cloak swirling in half circles each time he turned. His fair curls were darkened with sweat and it glistened in beads on his forehead. He was taller than Syrd and very slim. His face was stern, proud and arrogant. To the young people his magic was not in singing, like Syrd, nor in his words, like Andra, but in his power of leadership. But now Daëmon's blue eyes were brooding.

"It's not so much Andra herself that we need, but what she stands for."

"How d'you mean?" Syrd asked.

"Well, it's difficult to explain. She's a symbol of what we want to be. She's free."

"Andra is no more free than we are. She has to do what she's told just as we do."

"I know that, but she's free in her mind."

"Boy, you are beyond me. I just don't understand."

"You ought to, Syrd. You wrote Omyara. That's what Andra dangles in front of our noses, something vague, something we can't define. Freedom, Syrd. We don't even know what freedom is."

"Everything Administration says we can't have," Syrd muttered.

"In a sense, yes, but it's also something else which we seem to have lost through a few hundred generations, and something Andra has regained. Freedom is outside our thoughts, we're only just beginning to realise what it is and that's because Andra is telling us. But we can't have freedom because we're denied self-expression."

Syrd sighed.

"I'm still not with you. Self-expression? What's that?"

"Self-expression is Andra."

"Go on."

"Andra grows her hair long because she wants it that way. And why shouldn't she if she likes it? Personally, I think it looks awful but I've no right to make her wear it short just because I don't like it, nor has Shenlyn. Andra paints pictures she ought not to paint. She teaches you songs you ought not to sing. She rebels against society because she wants to be different and she tells us of a way of life that is beyond our conception, but even we in our apathy know it is far pleasanter than life in Sub-city One."

Daëmon reached the far wall to be confronted by a design in brilliant vermilion and gold. It was lurid in its brightness and he found himself thinking how much better were the quietly weird landscapes Andra painted. They should be here, where everyone could see them, not hidden away

146

in her room. He swung away from the ghastly fresco to see the white light from the ceiling reflected on the grey floor, giving the room an air of vastness and depth.

His voice echoed as he spoke.

"We can't choose the work we want to do. EDCO assigns us. We can't choose the colours of the clothes we wear because we are dressed according to our work. We are branded into social classes by the colour of our clothes and our IQ ratings. We never really know our parents, they're just people who visit us at EDCO and with whom we have tea now and then. We aren't even free to die when we want to. We're either expired at sixty or made to live on. We can't choose our own life partners, they're chosen for us by the computers. We've no ambition, no love, no happiness, no . . ."

"Don't keep on, boy. You're only saying what Andra said to Shenlyn on the way back. You're getting all worked up and it's no use. Shenlyn was too furious to listen. You sound like Jane Eyre."

"Yes," Daëmon agreed. "And the young ones will be wild tonight when they know Andra is not here to read to them. Andra feeds discontent into our minds just by reading *Jane Eyre*. That book is everything Sub-city One is not. Cromer would go purple in the face if he knew."

Daëmon turned again to wander back down the room.

"For heaven's sake sit down," Syrd snapped.

"You make me giddy. All this talk. You fill the air with fine words. There's no time for talk. We have to do something."

"Such as? Beat Shenlyn with a metal bar?"

Violence? Violence no longer existed. But a pulse beat wildly in Syrd's temple and anger made him hurl a chair across the room to clatter against the far wall with a harsh sound.

"That doesn't help much," Daëmon remarked.

"Phh! You've no guts, Daëmon. You talk and you talk, all those great noble words. But you *do* nothing. Shenlyn has ordered Andra to therapy. Are you just going to stand there and let her be rehabilitated?"

"I thought you told me Dr Lascaux wouldn't do it."

"Well, I've reconsidered. If Shenlyn ordered him to he would have to. I don't think even Dr Lascaux would openly defy Shenlyn. If you won't go and fetch her then I shall."

Daëmon grinned.

"Do you remember the first book Andra read? There was a knight on a white horse who rescued maidens in distress and got himself killed."

Syrd banged his fist on the table.

"Will you stop making me out to be a fool? I just want to get Andra out of therapy. It's not particularly that I want to rescue Andra, it's just that I am feeling an overwhelming pity for Dr Lascaux. He is a nice man, Daëmon, and Andra was mad, really wild. Think what Dr Lascaux must be going through right now."

Daëmon's grin turned to a chuckle, then his face became serious.

"OK. So I will go to therapy and get Andra for you. Will that make you happy?"

Syrd helped himself to a drink from the machine.

"I'll come with you."

"Oh no, Syrd. You'll be needed here tonight. You'll have to sing all the evening. Tell them Daëmon regrets Andra will not be here to read to them. Besides, it won't help anyone if you act without thinking. You might get us all landed under the electronic helmet. It is too soon to do anything rash. When Andra is back, then we will decide."

Syrd twanged a harsh note on the vinet.

"Maybe you are right. You realise that what you are about to do is open rebellion?"

"Yes, I do realise. I'm sticking my neck out for Andra. I wonder if it will be worth it."

Syrd sauntered towards the door.

"Probably," he said, "Andra will spit in your eye. And if you're not back at 2000 hours we shall come and fetch you."

I7

Daëmon was left alone. He stood on the corner watching Syrd disappear down the side street which led to their apartment. He wished Syrd was coming with him. To Syrd he could speak freely, but what would it be like talking to a stranger? And to Daëmon Dr Lascaux was a stranger. He walked away from the glass-fronted buildings which housed the people who belonged to the upper social circle, to take the street past the office blocks where the hum of computers came to him in gentle waves of sound. The streets themselves were deserted and Daëmon was acutely aware that he should not be here but working in the control room.

The sight of the purple uniform of a security patrol man was enough to send him scurrying into a side alley and hope he had not been seen. Now he hurried along the small streets between the rooms assigned to the menial workers which towered several storeys above him. Here there lived a thousand thousand people with an IQ much lower than his own. How unimportant and yet how necessary they were. Daëmon thought of them as he passed by, then dismissed them from his mind.

The door to mental therapy was made of clouded glass and glowed with the white light from beyond it. Daëmon was reluctant to enter. He had never been inside this building, he had never needed to go inside. This was where people went whose minds were deranged, people who could not face up to life or were filled with despair. It seemed to him that it was an admission of failure to enter mental therapy. He had no need for it and no time. He was young and strong, but so was Andra and yet she was here. He squared his shoulders and went inside.

The room was very big and almost empty. There was a child and a baby in arms with one of the personnel from the nursery. There was a man wearing the pale blue of Administration. There was a nurse behind the desk marked RECEPTION, another nurse talking to another nurse, and one at the filing cabinet in the corner. On a bench beside the door sat three people. They were middle-aged and their faces were quite expressionless. Their eyes stared at the blank yellow wall opposite them and their hands were clasped limply on their laps. Daëmon guessed they were here to be expired and fought down his desire to turn and run. Next year Fenner would be here staring stonily at that same wall. Not even the sound of someone screaming in another room flickered their unseeing eyes. Daëmon swallowed and walked towards the desk marked RECEPTION.

The nurse did not acknowledge his presence.

Her clothes were white and her eyes were mild as she looked round him and beyond him. She read from a card:

"Citizen C21/98/11 will go to room 307 in corridor B immediately."

One of the three sitting on the bench raised his head.

"Citizen C21/98/11 will go to room 307 in corridor B," the nurse repeated.

The man stood up. He was of medium height and his back was slightly bowed. He wore the dark red clothes of a factory worker. For the third time the nurse repeated the instruction and the man shuffled out.

Daëmon said:

"Can you help me? I wish to speak with Dr Lascaux."

She took a card from a pigeon-hole. It was tinted a pretty shade of pink and was titled in bold red letters ADMISSION. She did not even glance at Daëmon.

"You have attended therapy before?"

"No."

"Your annual psycho-check was carried out by whom?"

"Dr Bayco."

"Result?"

"Normal. Look, I don't know why you're asking me these things. I merely wish to speak with Dr Lascaux about a girl called Andra. I don't

152

know her number but she was brought here today."

The nurse appeared not to hear him.

"Your name and number?"

"Citizen C22/32/7: Daëmon."

"Intellect, routine or menial?"

"Intellect. IQ 138. Number of toes ten. Number of eyes 2. Diploma grade A in astrology, radar mechanics and nuclear physics. Now tell me where I can find Dr Lascaux."

"Do you suffer from: Loss of Memory? Debility? Lack of Concentration? Insomnia? Vertigo? Neurosis? Indigestion? Dandruff? Depression? . . ."

She went on and on. Daëmon said "yes" to them all and stared around him. This was all such a stupid waste of time. He was here to find Andra, not to answer the questions of this human computer. There were two people on the bench. The man from Administration was talking to a nurse and the other nurse was still working at the filing cabinet. She turned and smiled at Daëmon. He recognised her as one of the young people who came to the youth centre. He left the desk and almost ran across the room, vainly hoping he had remembered her name correctly.

"Hello, Daëmon. Are we losing you to therapy too? I didn't think you would ever need treatment."

"I don't. Maeia, where can I find Dr Lascaux?"

She regarded him for a moment. Her wide blue eyes were puzzled.

"Why? Daëmon, you aren't ill, are you?"

"No. It's Andra."

Maeia's eyes cleared.

"I wasn't here but Bandy told me. The whole place was in an uproar. Shenlyn himself came. Bandy was in a flap and Dr Linli nearly passed out. Bandy said Andra called Shenlyn some very rude names and she's got herself into frightful trouble. Daëmon, you can't go into therapy if there's nothing wrong with you. You have to be officially admitted."

"Maeia, dear, just tell me where to find Dr Lascaux. I'll officially admit myself. Dr Lascaux, Maeia, where is he?"

She said:

"Shenlyn asked for Dr Lascaux too. They couldn't find him. He has an afternoon of relaxation but we rang his apartment and he wasn't there. He might be in the medical lounge but we looked there too. Maybe he's come back and is with Andra."

"I'll try the medical lounge first. Where is it?"

"Corridor Q. Room 23."

"And Andra? Where's she?"

"I don't know," Maeia said.

Daëmon pulled the girl's white cap over her eyes.

"You are a dear, Maeia. I'll see you tonight."

He strode through the door at the far end. He

had not been officially admitted. The nurse from the reception desk called after him. Daëmon quickened his stride. When he looked back she was following him and Daëmon knew why Maeia had called her Bandy.

18

The phone trilled in the medical lounge. Automatically the man with grey-blue eyes picked it up.

"Yes?"

"I want to speak to Dr Lascaux."

"Kiroyo? This is Lascaux. Is something wrong?"

"Yes, everything is wrong. Lascaux, what did you do to Andra?"

"Andra? I haven't seen Andra since she left here over a year ago."

"Then I think you are about to make her acquaintance again. But it's that operation I was thinking about."

"The brain graft?"

"Yes, the brain graft. Tell me about it."

"It was just a simple graft. The psycho-visular regions."

"And you used the brain of a boy who died over two thousand years ago?"

"Who told you that?"

"Then it's true?"

"Yes. It is true. But I can't think why you're so suddenly concerned. The operation was a complete success."

"Mmm."

The clock on the wall swept past one minute.

"Kiroyo, are you still there?"

"I am still here. Lascaux, can I come and see you?"

"Of course. You know I will see you at any time. But why?"

"That little bit of brain you put in Andra's head . . . she remembers things that happened over two thousand years ago. She remembers what life was like on the surface of the earth."

"But that's impossible! Kiroyo, it's impossible. I never touched any other part of her brain, only the region of sight."

"Shall I reword it then? Shall I say she has seen life on the surface of the earth?"

"You are sure of what you are saying?"

"Quite sure. I should have come to you months ago when I first noticed."

"All right, Kiroyo, but I don't know what I can do about it. Come round, will you? I'll be in the lounge. I'll wait for you."

Lascaux dropped the phone. The conversation disturbed him but he had the report to finish so he pushed it to the back of his mind. It was less than ten minutes later when Linli came in, wiping his forehead with a tissue.

"You look hot and bothered," Lascaux remarked.

Linli helped himself to an iced drink. His hands were shaking.

"Shenlyn has been here," Linli muttered.

"Has he?"

"An hour ago. 1315 hours to be exact. I had just finished today's exterminations. He was furious."

"Was he?"

"It was that girl. Andra. You know, the one you did the brain graft on last year. She and Shenlyn, I've never heard anything like it. Never!"

Lascaux raised his eyes from the sheet of writing. He was becoming interested.

"Go on, Linli, tell me more."

Linli swallowed half a glass of the liquid.

"Shenlyn brought her in for therapy. He wanted her rehabilitated but Renson told him to cool down, she was too young for that. My hat! If I had been Shenlyn I would have told Renson to mind his own damned business. That girl would have definitely gone to the helmet. Shenlyn was livid, absolutely livid. She insulted him to his face. In front of everyone in Reception she called him a narrow-minded bore and a dithering nitwit. She told him he ought to have been expired a century ago. I simply didn't know what to do. Then she called him a pig. I don't know what 'pig' is but it sounded pretty frightful. I thought Shenlyn would blow up. It took three of us to get her to my consulting room. We almost carried her. Shenlyn wanted you to attend to her, but that stupid nurse couldn't find you. If I had known you were here . . ."

"Linli," said Lascaux, "just sit down for a moment and compose yourself. You say Shenlyn brought Andra in for therapy. How did Andra and Shenlyn happen to meet in the first place?"

Linli finished his drink.

"They went up to salvage the rocket. Kiroyo always goes up if there's a trip to the surface. This time he took Andra, and Shenlyn went too. That's how they met. Lascaux, you ought to see that girl. No wonder Shenlyn was riled. Just one look at her is . . ."

"Come in!" Lascaux commanded.

The door opened and the surgeon frowned.

"You have no business here. Who are you?"

"Citizen C22/32/7. Daëmon."

"Have you reported to Reception?"

"Yes, but I have not come for treatment. I wish to speak with Dr Lascaux. Where can I find him?"

Linli spluttered.

"Really! I don't know what Reception is coming to. If you have not come for treatment, kindly leave . . . immediately."

Daëmon did not move.

"I want to speak to Dr Lascaux," he repeated.

The surgeon held up his hand to the indignant Linli.

"I am Dr Lascaux, and this is highly irregular. What do you wish to speak to me about?"

"Andra."

"Come in and close the door. Pour yourself a drink if you wish, and be seated. No, Linli, don't protest. I know as well as you do that this young man should not be here but I wish to hear what he has to say."

Linli shrugged his shoulders and walked to the door. His manner was one of disapproval.

"Oh, by the way," Lascaux questioned, "where is Andra?"

"Room 37," snapped Linli. "I have sedated her for you and now I wash my hands of her."

The young doctor left the room.

The surgeon regarded the curly-haired youth. He wore dull gold colours which told Lascaux he worked in Space control. He was still standing. Lascaux indicated a chair but the boy shook his head.

"As you wish. Now, what do you want to tell me about Andra?"

Daëmon hesitated. Lascaux noted that his fists were clenched at his side.

"You came here to speak to me about Andra. What is it you wish to say?"

Very slightly Daëmon's chin moved upwards. His bearing was arrogant but he was decidedly good-looking. He gazed down on Lascaux with calm blue eyes. He had been dreading this moment, but now it was here he was no longer afraid. Even the silver badge which glowed on the surgeon's collar could not deter him.

"Dr Lascaux, you will not rehabilitate Andra."

Lascaux did not move. His eyes were a quiet grey-blue. Very slightly one eyebrow was raised and a bemused smile crossed his face as he drummed the desk with his fingers.

"You dare to give me an order?"

Daëmon's chin rose a little higher. It was too late to regret he had spoken.

"Yes, Dr Lascaux. I dare to give you an order. You will not rehabilitate Andra."

"And if I refuse to obey what will you do?"

"I am the youth leader of this city. Soon five hundred young people will know I have come. If I told them to come here they would come. They are very fond of Andra."

"Do I detect a subtle threat behind your words? If I place the electronic helmet upon your head the young people will be without a leader. Your threat is rather foolish."

"Not so foolish, Dr Lascaux. If you rehabilitate me they will be angry. I would not like to answer for what they might do."

Lascaux leant back in his chair. Daëmon thought his eyes were mocking him.

"I find your manner a little overbearing. Sit down! I said, sit down! You are lucky you chose me to make your ridiculous demands to and not Dr Massé. I am a far more tolerant person than my colleague, but even my tolerance has its limits. For your information, Andra is here for therapy, not rehabilitation."

Daëmon sat on the edge of the chair and stared at his hands. He had acted rashly and made a fool of himself, spoiled their chances of ever getting what they wanted, all to save Andra's wretched neck.

"I wish to apologise, Dr Lascaux," Daëmon murmured.

The surgeon leaned across the desk.

"You stick your neck out, Daëmon, do you not? I should report you for gross insubordination, but I am curious to know why you stick your neck out. Is Andra worth so much?"

"To us she is."

"Why?"

"Because she is right."

The chair creaked as Lascaux tipped it backwards. His fingers traced a line along the edge of the desk.

"So little Andra is right," he murmured. "She is right to abuse the Director of Sub-city One?"

Daëmon squirmed. How easy it was to twist words. "Come," Lascaux urged. "You tell me Andra is right. Why is she right?"

"Because she is free."

"But surely we are all free?"

Daëmon puckered his brow.

"Are we?"

"Of course," said Lascaux. "Of course we are free. We live in Sub-city One. We are clothed and fed. We have our work and our leisure. We are not imprisoned behind bars. We can roam through the gardens, dance in the dance halls, eat, drink and be merry. What more can we want?"

"Yes, we are free," Daëmon said sarcastically.

"Free as long as we do what we're told and don't speak out of place. That's not freedom. We can't leave the precincts of the city, we can't go to the surface without permission; we can't choose our life partners; we can't bring up our own children; free speech is non-existent; our leisure is limited by the rules of Administration; we can't choose the colours of our clothes; we can't choose our own apartments; we can't decorate them as we want. And we can't even die when we want to, we're just expired. Freedom is living, Dr Lascaux. We aren't living, we're just existing."

Lascaux was stunned.

"Is this what Andra has been saying?"

"Yes. And now I say it too."

The surgeon's eyes rested on the green curtain which covered the far wall.

"Many, many years ago Kiroyo said this would happen, and now it has come. The young people cry for change and I have a feeling it is all my fault."

Daëmon was curious and also relieved. Dr Lascaux did not seem angry.

"Would you say Andra was different from you?"

"Yes," Daëmon said. "She is different."

"And all these things you say you want, would you have thought of them if Andra hadn't put them in your mind?"

"Probably not," Daëmon admitted. "We have lived with these things so long that we have not

163

noticed them. We've accepted them as fact. Now Andra has told us of a better way of life and we have realised just how restricting are the rules of Administration. That's what I meant when I said Andra was right. She sees things as they ought to be."

" 'See' is an important word, Daëmon. What do you know about Andra?"

"I know she had a brain operation over a year ago. Syrd told me. I think it was a graft."

"It was," Lascaux confirmed. "And that is why Andra sees. If I had not operated she would have been blind. But the brain tissue which I used came from a boy who died over two thousand years ago. A few moments ago Professor Kiroyo phoned me. He informed me that Andra's eyes have seen another way of life. She has seen the times when a man chose his own wife. She has seen when men were free to walk where they liked on the surface of the earth, when they chose their work and their leisure, the colours and styles of their clothes. She has seen it and now she wants it for you. It has become impossible for her to accept conditions as they are in Sub-city One and so she tries to change it. For her it is a terrible tragedy because things can never be as she wants them."

Daëmon was silent.

"Kiroyo says it was I who made Andra what she is. I put that knowledge in her head. I could remove it. I could rehabilitate her."

Daëmon looked at him sharply.

"And will you?"

"I think it is a little late. She has already infected you with her dangerous ideas and besides, we have too many factory workers. No, Daëmon, I would never destroy the intelligence of a young girl. I condemned the electronic helmet a long time ago, but there are some who are liberal in using it."

Daëmon stole a glance around him. Previously he had seen only the face of the quiet man who confronted him, but now he saw the luxury: the gleaming metal fittings, the climbing plants, the plush upholstery, the carpet. This was an insight into the world of the upper social sector and the world he would enter if he took over from Fenner.

"I ought to regret that I came here," Daëmon said. "But I am glad I met you, Dr Lascaux."

The surgeon inclined his head.

"I will be watching with interest the activities of you young people. My sense of duty tells me I ought to inform Cromer of your attitude, but my sense of justice allows me to sit back and wish you luck. You side with Andra and I do not think you can win. Tread carefully, young man, you will have the disapproval of many people to contend with."

"And you will release Andra?"

"No, I will not release Andra. I have said I will sit back and watch you, but I will not join your revolution. Shenlyn has ordered Andra to undergo therapy and I will do as he asks. It may teach Andra a little respect. She will be here for at least six weeks and neither you nor your band of young people will force me to release her. I hope now we understand each other."

Daëmon rose and went to the door.

"I understand you, Dr Lascaux, and I also thank you for talking to me."

Daëmon opened the door and the old man from the archives stood there leaning on his stick. Daëmon bowed in silent respect.

"Come in, Kiroyo," Lascaux said. "Let me hear even more about Andra."

19

Daëmon wandered along the coloured corridors looking for the way back to Reception. The corridors were deserted and the doors closed. Now and then he heard voices behind the walls and frescoes blurred his vision. Lascaux had listened mildly to words that would have turned Cromer as purple as his tunic. And now Daëmon knew for certain that Dr Lascaux would never rehabilitate Andra, no matter what happened.

The blue walls changed to green, the near distance a blur of light to split into distinct shapes and become an open door. He saw her pacing the floor, to and fro, to and fro, looking down. Her black hair had been cropped short.

Daëmon leant against the lintel of the door.

"Hello, Andra."

She turned to face him, breathing heavily, her face white and furious. Then she scowled.

"Aren't you pleased to see me, Andra?"

She scowled again and went on walking.

"Why don't you sit down? You'll wear your boots out." She stopped suddenly.

"They cut off my hair."

It was said quietly, intense with hatred.

"It looks horrible," Daëmon said.

"Shenlyn cut off my hair," Andra said angrily. "I wish he was here now. I wish he was here."

Daëmon smiled.

"And what would you do if Shenlyn *was* here?"

"I'd make him wish he were dead. What are *you* doing here?"

"I came to see you."

"So now you've seen me why don't you laugh? I heard you up there, you and Syrd. I heard you laughing. They cut off my hair and you laugh. I get two whole months of therapy with misery-guts Linli and you laugh. Go away before I spit at you."

"Linli has refused to have anything more to do with you," Daëmon said placidly. "I feel sorry for Dr Lascaux."

"Huh! Why did you come to see me?"

"Actually, I didn't. I just happened to notice you on my way out. I came to see Dr Lascaux."

"What for?"

"About you. I told him he should not rehabilitate you."

"That was damned big of you. You might have asked him to let me out."

"I did."

"And he wouldn't?"

"He wanted to, but he wouldn't."

"Before long he'll be wishing he had."

"You ought to be grateful I came. At least it shows someone is concerned about you. Kiroyo is here too."

"Papa Kiroyo? Here for me?"

Andra's flashing eyes grew softer.

"He's with Lascaux now. Andra, you were an idiot to say all that to Shenlyn."

She sat down hard on the bed.

"I hadn't nearly finished. I'll make him glad to listen. He had my hair cut off. I'll make him sorry for that."

Daëmon sighed.

"And to go racing off like that when we were ready to leave didn't put him in a very good mood."

Her eyes were staring at him, big and brown and far away as if she didn't see him at all. Again he noticed how white her face was.

"You don't understand," Andra whispered. "Daëmon, you don't understand. For a moment it was all green, warm, heavy, singing green. It was everywhere mixed with the sun. If I could have reached him I need never have come back."

"You're darned right about that, Andra. You'd have been jam down on those rocks at the foot of the cliff."

"I didn't see the stupid cliff," she snapped, "not until Shenlyn grabbed me and it was all gone. How I detest that man. He is too conceited for words. He thinks he's a God. He'll regret he made me come here. He'll regret he ordered them to cut off my hair. I shall knock Shenlyn right where it hurts."

"Andra, don't do anything rash. You don't have

to go it alone. We'll all help you. We'll get the things we want."

She laughed and her thoughts were a thousand miles away. The things she wanted they would never have. They were gone and irretrievable. Maybe they could rake among the ruins and regain enough human independence to make Shenlyn realise he wasn't a God, but the trees and the fields and the greenness for which she longed would never come again. All she would have would be a moment of revenge.

Daëmon took her hand.

"Andra, wake up!"

Viciously she drew her hand away and pounded the wall.

"He is a pig. I hate him. Get them riled, Daëmon. Get them stamping mad. I'll be back and Shenlyn will squirm. He cut my hair and he'll . . ."

Daëmon shook his head.

"Andra, you can't rush a thing like this. You have to . . ."

"What the devil are you two doing here?" barked a voice. "You, girl, I know your face. Have we met before?"

"Dr Massé," Andra said. "Aren't you delighted to have me back?"

Daëmon beat a hasty retreat down the long green corridor. He could hear the loud grating voice of Dr Massé and the husky voice of Andra goading him to anger. She was so utterly strange:

it was green, warm, heavy, singing green, everywhere mixed with the sun. She didn't see the cliff. Her eyes had seen another way of life when men were free to go where they pleased on the surface of the earth. She made Daëmon worried and therapy would be in a turmoil whilst Andra was here.

CROMER

20

Syrd sat on the wall around the lake staring at the moving fish and the still reflections of bright red flowers. From the quiet plants round him he drew calmness and strength. Andra had changed since she returned from therapy six months ago. She was quieter, more intense. Now it was not so much the Sub-city she rebelled against as Shenlyn himself; Shenlyn, who had cut her hair. Shenlyn had probably forgotten all about the incident, but Andra hadn't. The past months had been months of waiting, months of preparation, building up to a climax: tonight, and the new song Andra had made him write. It was an outright attack on the Director and all he stood for. It was Andra's revenge.

Syrd realised that she had made him the figurehead of a revolution. He was the God the young ones worshipped, so Andra would use his music and his song and he would give her what she wanted, even a revolution. Grovinski meant nothing to him now, Grovinski was the past. Andra meant everything, she was the future, and the future began tonight.

He was startled when the image of Cromer appeared beside his own on the surface of the water: Cromer, the head of security, the cold ruthless man who had allowed Syrd to remain here. Cromer hadn't known he was a Uralian agent sent to crash the ship. No one had known that but himself. He had thought it was all over but the sight of Cromer made him remember, brought the vague unease rushing back to the surface. Cromer smoothed an imaginary crease in his immaculate purple uniform. The gold badge of rank was harshly prominent.

"You are enjoying our gardens?"

"Yes."

"You have made a very successful life for yourself here in our city."

"Yes."

"You have no commitments at the youth centre this evening?"

"I am going there now."

"Do you think that is wise?"

Syrd did not understand the question.

"Is it wise to fill your head with stupid songs? I hope your work will not suffer, nor music blind you to your other duty."

Cromer's words were strange. They had an undertone of something sinister. As if they had been carefully chosen to mean something else. The words of his instructor came rushing back. "You go to serve Grovinski. Always remember that. Your first duty in everything is for the superiority of the Uralian nation. That superiority must always be uppermost in your mind." Those words of Cromer's could have meant the same thing except that Cromer was head of security in Sub-city One. Syrd's knuckles gripping the edge of the wall were quite white.

Cromer smiled, a mechanical smile with no trace of sincerity in his cold blue eyes.

"Just remember that I watch you all the time, you and the youth leader and the girl from the archives who shares your room."

Syrd stood up, his heart pounding with anger and alarm.

"They are waiting for me," Syrd said. "I must go."

Cromer watched him. He hoped Syrd would not prove difficult.

Syrd went thoughtfully along the wide grey path and out into the great square in front of the Administration building. He glanced up at the towering façade of white plastic which reflected light like glass. A thousand thousand windows with a thousand thousand people working behind them. Why should Cromer watch them? Why should he watch Andra? To him she would appear just an ordinary girl. He hadn't heard the things she had said. He didn't know the thoughts that went on in her mind. He didn't know her hair had grown long again, long and black and beautiful. She was just a girl, an ordinary girl about to begin a rebellion. But Cromer couldn't know that so why should he watch her?

21

Andra pounded the computer, whirr click, whirr click, whirr click. "Damn!" She back-taped and started again: whirr click, whirr click, whirr click. She was impatient to be finished. Kiroyo watched her and wondered what was in the parcel the girl in the pink tunic had brought for her.

Andra slammed shut the book she had been working from and left the computer. Kiroyo patted the parcel.

"It is a present for me?"

"No. Not for you. You would look silly in a dress, Papa Kiroyo."

"A dress?"

"Yes. You know! A dress. Women used to wear them ages ago. A dress is like a tunic. It covers you. I will show you."

She went into the museum and closed the door. Kiroyo's brows were raised above his spectacles. A dress? Why on earth would Andra want a dress? Dresses hadn't existed for two thousand years. Where would she find a dress? He frowned. In the same place she had found a guitar? Stolen it from his museum? Persuaded the little lady from the factory to renovate it? But why would she want it?

Andra stood in the doorway. She was wearing the dress. It was made of dark blue shimmering material woven with silver threads in an intricate pattern of leaves. She had grown her hair again. It hung long and loose and black and she had fixed it with a shining glass flower. She looked like someone who had stepped from the pages of a book. Someone who belonged in that book, two thousand years back through time, not now.

Kiroyo leaned back in his chair as she came towards him. Her arms and legs were bare and the skirt swirled above her knees. She was smiling wickedly, a little witch with devilment in her eyes.

"Well, Papa Kiroyo? Don't you think it's pretty?"

"I think, my dear, it is a little exposing. But the material is indeed beautiful. Who made it?"

"Tarysa and Rina. They work in the design department. They design curtaining for the apartments of the upper social circle. They designed this for me."

Kiroyo nodded slowly.

"And now you have shown me your plaything, Andra, you may go and take it off. Also you will put the flower pin back where you found it. It is made of diamonds and very valuable, and I don't think they wore brooches in their hair."

"I am only borrowing it. I want to wear it tonight, Papa Kiroyo. I'll return it tomorrow."

Kiroyo leaned across the desk.

"You are not walking to the centre of the city looking like that?"

"I am."

"And if someone sees you?"

"I intend people to see me. I'll walk through the city in this dress. You will come with me, won't you, Papa Kiroyo?"

"Eh?"

The old man looked startled.

"Papa Kiroyo, you will come and dance with me? Ages ago you said you would. Have you forgotten?"

Kiroyo breathed on his spectacles.

"You surely don't expect me to be seen with you? You are not respectable. You show too much bare flesh, and besides, I have an important meeting with Shenlyn."

Andra laughed.

"Papa Kiroyo, you are just making excuses. I think you are a stuffy old man. Are you ashamed to be seen with me? Or afraid to be seen with me? Maeia has grown her hair long, so has Rina, so has . . ."

"Don't go on. Does Shenlyn know yet?"

"I think not."

Kiroyo stood up.

"So the thing has begun, Andra?"

"Yes, Papa Kiroyo, it has begun and maybe tonight it will end. Maybe tonight Shenlyn will know, and then your important meeting will be

180

abandoned anyway. So you see, you may as well come and dance with me."

So it had begun, the revolution had come. Kiroyo closed his tired eyes. So many years ago, nearly three hundred years ago, he had almost started one himself. He supposed everyone who had worked in the archives and worked among the books must have felt the same, but why did it have to be Andra who had boiled the bubble of unrest until it exploded? He gazed at her. Her dark eyes were glowing with luminous excitement. It had to be Andra, not because she had learnt to be different, but because she *was* different. She didn't belong here in Sub-city One. Dr Lascaux had brought her here through two thousand years of time.

He caught up his walking stick and took her arm.

"I am not afraid to be seen *with* you, Andra. But I am afraid *for* you, my dear."

22

For a while he would stay, but he would not dance. He was too old to dance. He would be an onlooker and watch the young ones. From his chair in the corner he could observe. They had hung Andra's paintings on the walls.

Syrd brought him a drink.

"Are you staying, Professor Kiroyo?"

"For a while, I think. I see Andra has brought her art out into the open."

"Daëmon and I like her paintings and the kids seem to. This is the first time they've seen them. They've had to imagine until now. You know she has read to us? Many books."

"She did not tell me. She steals without my permission, the guitar, my books. Where will it end? Where will Andra end? She fights a whole city, how can she win?"

"Not a whole city. Just Shenlyn."

"Shenlyn *is* the city."

"But she is not alone, Professor. We are with her. All of us. No one can break Andra's spirit."

"If she were rehabilitated, my boy, she would have no spirit. She would no longer be Andra but someone they made her into, a person with no mind. Is that what you want for Andra?"

The young people milled around them. Syrd watched them: five hundred different parts making one body and one mind. Unity!

"What they do to Andra we shall do to them. They will be destroyed, and Sub-city One as it is now will be destroyed. The young people are no longer automatons who do what they are told without question at all times. Andra has taught them to think and reason, and they do not like what she has taught their eyes to see. They are tired of Administration's restrictions. They rebel. We are ready, Professor Kiroyo, to march on Administration and demand the right to live, not merely exist. And now you know, will you tell Shenlyn?"

Kiroyo shook his head.

"No," he said simply. "Shenlyn will find out for himself before long. He will find out so many things and Andra will too. You see, Syrd, both Andra and Shenlyn are right but they are also wrong. I doubt very much if we shall ever find the happy medium."

"I don't understand."

"Andra is right: we do need freedom. Shenlyn is also right: we do need laws. Andra wants a world without laws. Shenlyn wants a world without freedom. It would be better to have something in between. A continuation of what we have with a little more of what is desirable."

Syrd realised that Kiroyo was a wise old man, older and wiser than Andra. Kiroyo watched as

Andra led them to chase a dream, a flash of colour in her mind, an echo through the passages of time, like Omyara which Syrd had written for her when it all began, something that would slip away before they caught it. Syrd forced his way between the mass of bodies. They were calling for him to sing and he would sing . . . for Andra.

"And we won't be computered or confined,
And we won't be restricted or assigned.
We'll speak the thoughts in our minds:
We'll be free, we'll be free, we'll be free."

They could clap to it, stamp to it, shout with it, sing with it, chant it, catch the rhythm: Syrd's new song, their song, a war song. Kiroyo sighed as the young ones screamed to hear it again. If Shenlyn heard it he would commit murder and murder hadn't been committed for hundreds of years. But Andra wanted more than singing.

The silence was loud and sudden. Five hundred young people sat cross-legged on the floor and stared. It was as if they had never seen Andra before. Her arms and legs were bare and her dress was shimmering blue, silver where the silver threads caught the light. But Andra herself amazed them even more. Her cloak and cap were gone. Her hair fell around her, long, gleaming and utterly black. They hadn't known her hair was black. Andra was like some being from a far-off star.

Then her voice came to them, familiar, low and husky, rising and falling, bringing magic which took them away from the walls and passages to the wide open spaces and the sun. They had listened to her before, almost every evening for twelve long months, and every evening the scar of regret Andra's voice left behind was a little deeper. But tonight it was not a story Andra told them.

"The world of books has gone. The wild things, the green things, the living things have gone. Nothing can ever bring them back. There is only one thing left, one living thing that survived. Human people lived on below the surface of the earth from generation to generation, through two thousand years of time, to you and me."

Her brown eyes swept over the blue ones which stared up at her. Soon, very soon, Shenlyn was going to be sorry he'd had her hair cut off.

"How much have we changed?" Andra asked. "How much have we lost of ourselves and how much have we got left? All the independence of Scarlett O'Hara, all the sadness and cruelty of Cathy, all the gentleness and love of Jane have gone. There is nothing left, neither hate nor love, cruelty nor kindness, sadness nor happiness. There is nothing left. No ambition, no achievement, no expression. Nothing. This Sub-city we live in, it's like a computer, a huge oversize computer with a Director who sits there and flicks the controls. It's nothing. So are we. Our heads are quite empty because we never think about anything. So it's time we did think, and talk, about this place and about Shenlyn."

She glanced briefly at Syrd and Daëmon who stood beside her on the platform. There was not a sound in the room. Not a movement.

"Who is Shenlyn?" Andra asked.

No one answered her.

"Shall I tell you who Shenlyn is? Shenlyn is Administration. Shenlyn is security, mental therapy, rehabilitation, EDCO, the colour of our clothes, the rules, the restrictions. Shenlyn is Subcity One. Shenlyn makes us what we are. Things without minds. Am I right?"

Kiroyo waited for someone to answer her.

"Let's answer her," Daëmon said. "Is Andra right?"

"Yes," someone said.

"Yes," came the muttered chorus.

"Yes," Andra said. "I am right. Tarysa, if you loved Daëmon and the computer found you incompatible could you live with him?"

A chuckle of amusement rippled through the room. A girl in the front row blushed. Daëmon held up his hand.

"Could you live with me, Tarysa, if the computer found us incompatible?"

"No."

It was hardly audible.

"Why not?" Daëmon asked.

The answer came stronger.

"My IQ would be graded lower than yours and Administration would not allow it."

"Shenlyn would not allow it," Andra corrected. "Shenlyn *is* Administration."

"Maeia, if you had a green dress could you wear it?"

Maeia looked surprised.

"Of course not."

"Why not?"

"Shenlyn would not allow it. I work in therapy so I have to wear white."

"And Tarysa, could you make Maeia a green dress?"

"No."

"Why not?"

Tarysa was silent.

"Answer her," Daëmon commanded. "Why couldn't you make a green dress for Maeia?"

"Because Maeia works in therapy and I'd have to make her a white one."

"But you made me a blue one," Andra pointed out.

"I didn't know you'd wear it," Tarysa muttered. "I thought . . ."

"And why shouldn't I wear it?" Andra demanded. "Why shouldn't I wear a blue dress? Just because I work in the archives and Shenlyn demands that people in the archives wear silver? Why should we be branded into social classes by the colour of the clothes we wear? If you work in the factories you wear red or pink. If you work in

Administration you wear pale blue. Everyone knows your IQ's low if you wear red or pink. Everyone knows your IQ's high if you wear blue. Why can't we wear any colour we want to wear? Pink, or blue, or yellow, or red? Why can't we grow our hair long and let everyone see it's long? Well . . . why can't we?"

Some said loudly:

"Because Shenlyn won't let us."

Andra smiled.

"Because Shenlyn won't let us. Louder!"

"Because Shenlyn won't let us!!!"

"And you can't spend your life with the person you want to because you have to go through computer tests. You have your life partners chosen for you by a computer. What kind of union is that, for heaven's sake? It's *your* life. Why should you be told by a computer who you must live with? Why can't you choose for yourself? Why can't you love? Well. . . why can't you?"

"Because Shenlyn won't let us!"

"Louder!"

"Because Shenlyn won't let us!!!"

"Maeia, do you like working in therapy?"

"No."

"Then why do you work there?"

"I was assigned there from EDCO."

"So you spend the rest of your life doing work you hate because you were assigned there? What kind of life is that? Why should you be told what work you have to do? Why can't you choose for yourself? Why can't you do the work you choose to do? Well . . . why can't you?"

"Because Shenlyn won't let us!"

"Louder!"

"Because Shenlyn won't let us!!!"

"So you think there's something wrong with this place? Well . . . do you?"

"Yes!!!"

"You're darned right there's something wrong. There's no freedom. All the time you have to do what you're told. And if you don't like it that's just your hard luck. You can't protest because if you did you'd be rehabilitated. You can't write about it because it would never pass the censor. You can't hold a meeting to discuss it even, because security wouldn't allow it. Why can't you stand in Administration Square and say what you want to say? Well . . . why can't you?"

"Because Shenlyn won't let us!!!"

"Louder!"

"Because Shenlyn won't let us!!!!"

It rose to a shriek.

"Right. Let's quicken it up. Can you live past sixty if your IQ is under 100?"

"No."

"Why not?"

"Because Shenlyn won't let us!"

"Oh, louder than that!"

"Shenlyn won't let us!!!"

"Can you visit your parents without getting a pass from EDCO?"

"No!"

"Let everyone hear you. Why not?"

"Because Shenlyn won't let us!!!"

"When you have children of your own can they live with you?"

"No!"

"Why not?"

"Because Shenlyn won't let them!"

"They're brought up at EDCO!"

"And if you want to call Cromer a fool, can you?"

"No!!"

"Why not?"

"Because Shenlyn won't let us!!!"

"Can you go anywhere on Earth you want to go?"

"No!!"

"Why not?"

"Because Shenlyn won't let us!!!"

"Can you leave Sub-city One if you want to?"

"No. We can't even do that!"

"Why not?"

"Because Shenlyn won't let us!!!"

It was becoming a kind of chant. They could stamp their feet, clap their hands, and the questions went on, and the answers went on, louder and louder, filling them with a sense of power and rage. They wanted to go out in the streets and shout: Shenlyn won't let us! Shenlyn won't let us!

190

It made them laugh. It made them sad. It filled them with fury.

"You can't do a bloody thing," Andra shouted. "And why not?"

"Because Shenlyn won't let us!!!!"

"So what's wrong with this place?"

"Everything!"

"Shenlyn!!"

"Shenlyn!!"

"What's wrong with this place?"

"Shenlyn!!!!"

"And what do we want?"

There was a pause. Kiroyo rose to his feet and made for the door. It was time he parted company with these young ones before the stampede towards Administration started. He was too old to march with them, too old for the excitement and the violence of their mood.

"What do we want?" Andra demanded impatiently.

"Tarysa wants to live with Daëmon," Maeia said. "And I don't want to work in therapy. Kids . . . what do we want?"

"No more therapy!"

"Destroy the electronic helmet!"

"Social distinctions out!"

"Long hair!"

"Free speech!"

"Home life! No EDCO!"

"The end of the Directorship!"

"Security abolished!"

"No computers!"
"Shenlyn out!"
"What do we want?"
"Shenlyn out!!"

The room was in an uproar. There was laughter and shouting. There was Andra on the platform with flying hair. There were cat-calls, whistling and war-whoops, and they all wanted Shenlyn out. Syrd strummed the guitar, Andra and Daëmon started clapping. The young ones caught the rhythm and the song Syrd had sung earlier came again. This time they understood the meaning. This time they meant the words they sang.

"And we won't be computered or confined.
And we won't be restricted or assigned,
We'll speak the thoughts in our minds:
We'll be free, we'll be free, we'll be free."

23

"Where's Kiroyo?" Shenlyn asked Cromer.

"I have no idea."

"He's late. He ought to have been here half an hour ago."

"Perhaps he's still working," Renson suggested.

"It is 2100 hours. He shouldn't be working at this time of night."

"Well, he's not here, is he?" Cromer commented drily and poured himself another drink. "Can't we eat without him? He's probably forgotten and gone to his apartment. Kiroyo is an old man, Shenlyn."

Shenlyn did not need Cromer to remind him of something he already knew. Kiroyo was 307 years old, to be exact. He might be very old but he didn't forget. The Director took up his cloak and went to the door.

"Kiroyo should be here. It is pointless to proceed without him."

"Are you intending to go and find him?" Cromer inquired.

"I am."

Cromer put down his drink and stood up.

"Can't your film show wait until the morning?" Shenlyn swung round.

"No, it can't. I want Kiroyo here and I want him now. Renson, order our meal to be ready in half an hour."

The Director of Sub-city One swung down the corridor, and Cromer followed him with an irritated frown: through the double doors of the rear exit and out into the gardens. Cromer cast a disinterested glance over the tangle of plants deepened from green to dark blue under the dim light. There was a drip, drip of water over the pool and far away the hiss of a fountain. All this frippery was so unnecessary. What was the use of a great ornamental garden which glazed the eyes of the working people? For the upper social class maybe it was pleasant, but working people had no need of it. Erase it and build. This was valuable space wasted and Kiroyo wasn't there.

Cromer gnawed his nails as they swung round to the front of the Administration building into the main Square. Here the light was brighter. So one spool of film had survived the crash and had been complete enough for the scientists to reconstruct it. It had taken them six months to reproduce it, but they had done it. And Shenlyn would not run through it without Kiroyo. Cromer's curiosity was intense and he found the Director's habits very frustrating at times.

Shenlyn paused in the centre of the Square, uncertain which way to go.

"His apartment?" Cromer suggested. "It would be much easier to phone."

"A walk will do you good," Shenlyn replied.

So Cromer found himself taking an evening stroll with Shenlyn past the community rooms, the lower class theatre and dance rooms towards the apartments of the upper social circle. They heard music, at first faint and far away, but coming clearer with every step they took.

"The young people are in high spirits tonight," Shenlyn remarked.

Cromer grunted. He didn't like young people. He tolerated them as necessary but he didn't like them. Their laughter and their singing grated on his ears, filling him with an unreasonable irritation. It sounded like a primitive war dance: clap, clap, clap, Shenlyn out! Clap, clap, clap, Shenlyn out!

"And why haven't you stopped them?" Shenlyn inquired calmly.

Cromer glared.

"Because I was with you in your apartment, Shenlyn, waiting for Kiroyo, who I now see walking away from us along the street."

"And your patrol men? Why haven't they taken some action?"

"That I can't tell you until I ask them."

They halted outside the doors of the youth centre.

"Stop them now," Shenlyn growled.

The head of security swung through the glass doors into the room and behind him came the Director of Sub-city One. No one noticed they were there except the girl on the dais. She inclined her dark head to acknowledge their presence and went on singing. Her arms and her legs were bare. Her dress was deep blue and shimmered in the light and in her hair she wore a white flashing flower. And her hair was long. Cromer was nauseated by the sight. Shenlyn was enraged.

"Stop!" he bellowed.

But they were all singing and they didn't hear. The girl ignored them.

The song went on and she did not look their way again:

"And we won't be restricted or confined,
And we won't be computered or assigned.
We'll speak the thoughts in our minds:
We'll be free, we'll be free, we'll be free."

The chorus faded away and two more security men joined Cromer and Shenlyn. There was no way for them through the crowd.

The girl on the dais straightened her shoulders.

"Are we free to do what we want?"

"No!!"

'Why not?"

"Because Shenlyn won't let us!"

"Are we free to go where we want?"

"No!!"

"Why not?"

"Because Shenlyn won't let us!"

"What do we want?"

"Shenlyn out!"

"Free choice!"

"Ballot vote!"

"The end of depression!"

"The end of restrictions!"

"The end of directorship!"

"Shenlyn out!"

"Again! Louder! What do we want?"

"Shenlyn out!! Shenlyn out!! Shenlyn out!!!"

There was a slight pause and the dark laughing eyes were triumphant.

Shenlyn took his chance.

"You, you and you: report to therapy. Cromer: escort them. The rest of you take down those designs from the walls and return to your rooms."

The hush in the room was heavy and no one moved. They did not even turn their heads to see who was behind them. Two more men in purple uniforms entered. Cromer felt a desire to wring their necks. He had not realised it had reached this stage. He had sat back and watched it happen but it had progressed so fast. The small unrest had grown into a revolution since the girl from the archives had returned from therapy six months ago. He had been watching her. He had known what she was doing. He had been waiting for her to overstep the mark, to show her rebellious nature openly. Now she had, and Shenlyn was here to see. It was the end of her little bid for independence, but, more important, it was the end of Andra herself.

He pressed the red button beside the door. The alarm buzzer sounded briefly throughout the city.

"You two boys on the platform, and you, girl, will come with me," Cromer snapped.

Still no one moved.

Cromer pushed through the crowd and the security men followed him. The girl was laughing. How dare she laugh in his face? He heard his men running along the street, the pound of their feet making a hollow sound. There would be enough men now to deal with this little uprising. Cromer reached up and grasped the girl's hair. There was an angry hum around him as he pulled her from the dais.

"Take your hands off me," Andra shrieked. "Take your hands off me!"

Cromer's cloak was pulled from behind, nearly choking him. He released the girl and swung round in fury. The material ripped. Young people were all round him with silent angry eyes.

"Let me through," Cromer said quietly.

The circle tightened, threatening, menacing. He looked across their heads and nodded.

"Clear a way!"

There was a noise, angry shouting, scuffling. The security men came from the street to force the young people back. Cromer watched, sardonically smiling until someone struck him under the eye and sent him reeling. He gripped Andra's arm and made her walk between the purple wall of men who held back her friends. Syrd and Daëmon were standing by the door with their arms pinioned behind their backs. Andra walked with her head held high. Cromer hurled her towards Shenlyn. That girl needed to be taught humility. He wished he could teach her. Her whole appearance disgusted him and his eye was beginning to swell.

Shenlyn regarded her grimly.

"Lady, you and I have met before. I recall our last meeting was also unpleasant. That time I was persuaded against my better judgment to be lenient with you. This time your hair will be removed by the roots and you will be rehabilitated. Take her away!"

"No," Syrd said. "You can't do that!"

Cromer's upper lip curled.

"You speak out of place, boy! Move! Now!"

The security men who held Syrd and Daëmon forced them into the street. Cromer spun round to face the sudden surge of movement behind him, the howl of anger which came like a cry from a single throat.

"Get out!" Cromer said to Shenlyn. "I'll deal with this."

The barrier of security men held them back whilst the Director left the room. The young people screamed at him. Andra, Syrd and Daëmon had been taken away and they couldn't reach them. There were too many men to break through. The anger died away and left silent horror behind.

"You will leave one at a time," Cromer instructed them, "and go to your apartments. This centre will be out of bounds to you all for at least six months. The streets will be patrolled by security men tonight and every other night until order is restored. Anyone leaving their apartments after 2000 hours will be rehabilitated and public meetings in any place are forbidden. All girls who have grown their hair long will have it trimmed to a respectable length before they report for work tomorrow. I hope we understand each other. Now you may leave, one at a time."

The room began to empty.

"Take down those paintings," Cromer instructed one of his men. "All of them. I will incinerate them myself."

24

They had spent the night together in the small square room. The bunks had been hard and they had not slept much. Andra lolled in apparent unconcern against the pillows watching the blue light turn to white again and knowing it was the start of another day. On the bunk above, Syrd leaned over to see if she was still asleep. Daëmon sat cross-legged on the floor frowning in concentration.

"This is utterly ridiculous," Daëmon concluded. "I don't need mental therapy. What's it like anyway?"

"Psycho-analysis," Andra told him. "They ask you questions and you answer them. Then they ask you the same questions slightly reworded and again you answer them. Then they reason with you. They go on for days and days. At the end you are supposed to think that Shenlyn is a God and Sub-city One is Paradise or else you simply run out of arguments to convince them that the whole place is crummy and Shenlyn is a pig. It's all completely pointless and if it's Massé who's doing the talking it's best to keep your mouth shut. He's too conceited to argue with. Linli you can tie up in knots quite easily, and Dr Lascaux you can hold a pleasant conversation with."

Syrd knew what Andra meant, but it was immaterial what happened to himself and Daëmon. For Andra it was going to be different.

"And rehabilitation?" asked Daëmon. "What's that? What is this helmet thing everyone talks about?"

Again it was Andra who answered him, her eyes staring at the yellow wall.

"The electronic helmet? I asked Dr Lascaux last time I was here. They fix it over your head and plug it into the computer. There are little wires which are padded to your skull and all your intelligence is pumped out and the computer pumps some more back in. Apparently you end up just like a baby. You've no memory and you can't even think. They have to teach you all over again how wonderful this ant-hill we live in is and this time you believe them because you can't reason for yourself that they're wrong."

Syrd swung himself to the floor.

"And is that what they intend for you?"

"I believe so."

"But they can't do that."

Daëmon raised his head.

"And they won't," he stated.

"Your darned right they won't," said Andra.

"But what can we do? The kids won't come without one of us there to urge them on."

Daëmon smiled.

"Sometimes, Syrd, I wonder how you came to

be credited with an IQ of 127. They won't rehabilitate Andra because she won't be here."

"What?"

"The next time that door opens, we leave."

"Daëmon, you're a genius," Andra said. "Even I hadn't thought of that."

It was two hours later when Dr Linli unlocked the door. He backed into the room, saying to the man behind him:

"Citizen C22/32/7 will go to Rawmann in Room 93 so if you wish to remain in this room it's vacant. I'm taking the girl. Lascaux and Massé are operating."

"Good morning, Dr Linli," said Daëmon as he walked past.

Syrd escaped with a mere nod of his head.

Linli was surprised. He said: "Good morning," then he realised. He realised in time to grasp Andra.

"Stop them: those two boys."

Andra squirmed and the shining material of her dress slipped from his fingers. He caught her wrist. Confound Daëmon! Why hadn't he been quicker?

"Leave them," Linli muttered. "Help me with this girl. She is more important. She must be rehabilitated immediately."

Syrd and Daëmon had reached the end of the corridor before they realised Andra wasn't with them.

"Go back?" asked Syrd.

"No! Syrd, in here, quickly! Look who's coming."

Out of the blur of light came a tall thin man in a purple uniform. It was unmistakably Cromer. Daëmon disappeared and Syrd followed him to close the door and face the man on the bed who stared at them. Footsteps passed by the door.

"Good morning," Daëmon said. "I am glad you are progressing satisfactorily. Dr Linli asked me to look in on you."

The man nodded his head and smiled.

They could no longer hear footsteps in the passage outside.

"Idiot!" Syrd commented. "Did Cromer see us?"

"He might have done," replied Daëmon, "but if he didn't he'll soon know we're missing. The sooner we get out of this building the better."

"But what about Andra? We can't leave her here."

"With three men against us, probably more, we don't stand a chance. We'll have to do a round-up. All the young people you can find. Fetch them here quickly. The processing factory is the nearest. You go there. I'll try design. Tell them to leave their work and come here."

Daëmon nodded pleasantly to Bandy as they ran through Reception and down the steps to the street.

"Be quick!" he said to Syrd as they parted.

* * *

Linli and his assistant had dragged Andra as far as the computer room when Cromer joined them.

"Trouble?" Cromer inquired.

"Yes," panted Linli. "The boys have gone and the girl defies us. She won't obey the simplest instruction."

Cromer pointed to the chair.

"Sit down, girl!"

She stood with her back against the wall, her hair falling about her and her eyes wild. She would not obey even Cromer.

"I said: sit down," Cromer snapped.

"Sit down, Andra," Linli pleaded. "I can't fix the helmet on your head whilst you're standing up. Sit down. It won't hurt you."

"You must think I'm stupid. I know what that thing does. I've seen the sort of people it turns out: dimwits."

Cromer said in a cold voice:

"Shenlyn has ordered you to be rehabilitated and rehabilitated you will be."

"There's nothing I can do about it," Linli said.

"It staggers me how you ever graduated, Linli," Andra said as she ran her hands through her hair. "If you won't do anything there's plenty I can do. You are not putting that thing on my head."

"There's no need to be rude," said Linli, feeling peeved. "Nor is there any need to be difficult."

Cromer was becoming impatient. The two boys didn't matter, but this girl did. She had to be destroyed.

"If you won't sit down we shall have to make you."

"You can try," she replied coolly.

Cromer took a step towards her. This girl would be rehabilitated now before she could do any more damage.

"Don't touch me, Cromer."

The curt order stung Cromer. Who was she to give him orders? She faced him calmly as he advanced.

"I warn you: don't touch me."

Cromer smiled. One more step and he could grip the nerve centre of her neck. She would be glad then to sit down. One more step. He took it and she lashed out at him. Something stabbed his arm, raking deeply through the skin. The sharp pain made him recoil. Linli watched in horror as the blood rushed from the gash in Cromer's arm. The spurt of a severed artery spilt on the floor in a red pool. Cromer's face turned green.

"You . . ."

"Savage?" Andra suggested. "Cat? Bitch? If you wish to be crude there are many words. Use your imagination, Cromer."

The medical orderly who was assisting Linli applied a tourniquet to Cromer's arm as he sank on to the chair beside the computer. She watched without a flicker of shame as Linli dressed the wound.

"It needs stitching, Cromer."

"Later. Let's attend to our little friend first.

Violence, Linli. Violence! You see how badly warped her mind is."

Cromer hauled himself to his feet. His blood was all over the computer and his uniform was stained brown.

"Sit her on the chair," Cromer instructed the medical orderly. "Linli, help him."

Linli approached Andra warily.

"Be careful," Cromer warned. "She has scalpels instead of nails."

Again Andra lashed out and caught the back of Linli's hand. It was only a small scratch but enough to bleed. He sucked at it and Andra opened her hand. In her palm a white glass flower flashed fire and Linli could see the sharp pin which had pierced his skin.

"Papa Kiroyo's diamond brooch," Andra informed him. "It is a jewel of the past, a mere adornment, but I'm very glad I borrowed it."

Cromer pressed the buzzer on the wall and two more orderlies answered it.

"Sit her down," Cromer instructed them heavily. The bandage on his arm was red. It throbbed with escaping blood and he felt his legs turn to water. "Put that girl under the helmet," Cromer said again as he slumped to the floor.

She fought like an animal in a trap. They would take away her mind and she would not let them. The walls of the room were spotted with blood but they were four men and she was only a girl.

"Dr Lascaux," Andra screamed. "Dr Lascaux! Dr Lascaux, help me!"

Lascaux had almost finished the brain transplant. Vallonde would live again as Shenlyn had requested. The spinal column and the optic nerves had been joined. One man had ceased to exist and another had taken over his body. Lascaux straightened his aching back and heard someone calling him. Someone was standing behind him. He swung round. There was only a nurse by the instrument table. He turned again to the man on the table. Last time he had done a major brain operation it had been Andra. It had turned her hair from fair to dark and her eyes from blue to brown. He sensed that someone was calling him.

He peeled off his gloves.

"Finish it," he told Massé.

"But you can't leave now, Lascaux. This is your patient, not mine."

"Finish it. There's something wrong somewhere. Someone called me."

"Don't be absurd, Lascaux. This room is sound-proof."

"Someone called me," Lascaux insisted. "Just carry on, Massé. Join the carotid artery. I'll be back soon."

He left the team of nurses round the table to go from the white-hot room and fling his smock and cap on the nearest chair. As he entered the corridor he heard someone calling his name.

"Dr Lascaux, please come! Please come!"

Lascaux shook his head. Either his ears were deceiving him or that was Andra. She called again and he almost ran to the computer room. There he took in the scene with a quick glance: Linli, the orderlies, the blood on the walls, Cromer slumped on the floor and the girl squirming under the electronic helmet.

"What the hell's going on?"

Cromer muttered something. Linli wiped the sweat from his face. On the floor sparkled a white stone flower.

"Thank goodness you've come," said Linli. "I can't do anything with her. How can I attach the wires when she won't sit still?"

"Just what do you think you're doing, Linli?"

"I am going to rehabilitate her."

"You are going to do what?"

Lascaux's usually calm temperament was ruffled.

"What did you say you were going to do, Linli?"

"Rehabilitate her. Shenlyn ordered it. Cromer has come to see that the order is carried out."

"Release her immediately!"

"But Shenlyn . . ."

"Release her, Linli. Release her now."

Cromer staggered to his feet and swayed unsteadily. Blood still trickled from his bandaged arm.

"That girl is to go to the helmet," he gasped.

"She is to be rehabilitated now. Lascaux, that is an order."

"And in mental therapy," said Lascaux, "it is I who give the orders, not you, Cromer. Your department is security."

"It is Shenlyn's order. You must obey."

"So if Shenlyn stormed in here in one of his tempers that is nothing to do with me. What does Shenlyn know about the workings of the human mind? Nothing! Not a damned thing! I will not be responsible for destroying this girl's intelligence."

Linli took the helmet from Andra's head and loosened the clips from her arms.

"What do I tell Shenlyn?" he asked as Cromer's knees gave way for the second time.

Andra crossed to the surgeon's side. He put his arm around her shoulder and felt her body shaking. Her bare arms were as cold as ice. She had been badly frightened.

"Tell Shenlyn that she doesn't need rehabilitating. Tell him . . . no, never mind. I'll tell him myself. You had better dress the wounds of the head of our security system. He might be needed and by the look of the amount of blood on the walls of this room he also requires a transfusion. Come with me, Andra. What have you done this time to displease Shenlyn? Or should I say what has Shenlyn done to displease you?"

He bent and picked up the diamond brooch.

"What's this?"

"That," said Linli, "is the weapon Andra used to attempt a dissection of Cromer's forearm and the back of my hand. I believe Mikam too had a mild taste of it. She tells us it is Professor Kiroyo's diamond brooch."

Lascaux pinned it to Andra's dress.

"It looks pretty dangerous. Just like you, Andra."

25

Renson switched on the light.

Shenlyn said:

"Well, Kiroyo, now you've seen it what do you think? Yes or no?"

Kiroyo was taken aback.

"Are you thrusting the decision on to me, Shenlyn? I thought you'd already made up your mind."

"Theoretically I have," Shenlyn agreed, "but the practical possibility is beyond me. It's a question of knowledge which I don't possess. You do, so I ask you again: is it possible?"

Kiroyo sank deep into his armchair and the men in the room on the top floor of Administration waited for him to speak.

"I don't know," Kiroyo said. "My sight tells me it is and my instinct tells me it is. On the face of things I would say yes, it is possible. Planet 801 should easily support a community. But I think, my friend, you asked me the wrong question."

Shenlyn wondered what the old man meant.

"The question should not have been is it possible, but *how* is it possible?"

"How *is* it possible?" Shenlyn repeated.

"That is what I don't know."

"But you must!"

"Not for sure. I recognise some of the plant life as similar in form to that which existed on this earth two thousand years or more ago. With research and study of the film I could tell you the soil conditions and the climate, and the geological structure, and the species of animals and the food content of the plants, but it will take me months, maybe years of searching among the books in my library."

Shenlyn strode across the room.

"I can't wait months or years, Kiroyo. I want to know now. The ships are ready. Why wait years when we can leave almost immediately? Kiroyo, you must know."

The telephone trilled in the next room and Renson was called away. Kiroyo shook his head. The light gleamed weirdly on his spectacles.

"I'm sorry, Shenlyn. I do not know. I have not the memory of a computer. I can find out but I don't know. You must be patient, my friend. You can't transport a thousand young people to that planet. They will die if they are not first taught how to live there. They must be prepared for a life so different that they are unable even to imagine it. Some plants may be poisonous. There is disease. In places the weather will be treacherous. There are carnivorous animals. They will die unless they are taught. And who will teach them? Myself? Maybe after five years of delving among my books to refresh my memory I could teach them, but it seems you are not prepared to wait five years."

"No, I'm not prepared to wait five years."

"Then you must ask Andra."

Renson returned as Shenlyn whirled round. "His cloak flies like a bat's wing," Kiroyo thought, "and he frowns like a vulture. I think my little Andra made him very angry last night."

"What did you say, Kiroyo?"

"Ask Andra, Shenlyn. She will recognise what I will not. She has seen the plants and the animals. She saw the world before it died and she will know how to live on planet 801. Through the eyes Dr Lascaux gave her, the eyes of the boy Richard Carson, Andra has seen these things. And believe me, she will remember them."

Shenlyn gripped the back of a chair.

"You are exposing yourself as a fool, old man. For three hundred years you have studied only to admit that a child knows more than you. I don't believe you, and your assistant was rehabilitated an hour ago."

Kiroyo's face drained to an ashy whiteness. He bent his head and Shenlyn permitted himself to feel a small sorrow for the old man. Kiroyo had become fond of the girl. He had been foolish to become fond of her and now she was gone he would grieve.

Renson cleared his throat.

"Kiroyo, will this girl really be able to help?"

Kiroyo turned his head to look, not at Renson, but at the Director of Sub-city One.

"Not now," he said. "Not now. She will be as useless as a piece of office furniture. Andra is gone and the body that remains cannot help us. I renounce my badge of rank and my social position. I also renounce my life. You will not rejuvenate me again. Find another to start again the research in the archives. You have destroyed a human girl and I spit upon your stupidity."

Renson put a restraining hand on the old man's arm.

"Don't be too hasty, Kiroyo. Dr Lascaux was on the phone a moment ago. He gave me a message for our Director. The message went as follows: tell Shenlyn that the next time he pokes his nose on my territory I shall try the electronic helmet on *his* head. I hope it will fit. There is nothing wrong with the mind of Kiroyo's assistant and I refuse to rehabilitate her."

Shenlyn stiffened.

"There was also a message from the girl which I am reluctant to repeat."

"Tell us," Kiroyo demanded. "Tell us what Andra said."

Renson glanced at Shenlyn.

"Shenlyn, you rotten pig, I will make you sorry. I will get you for this."

The room was utterly silent. Only the soft purr of the film projector and the sound of their own breathing could be heard. Then Kiroyo chuckled.

215

Renson said:

"Dr Lascaux also informed me that Cromer had severed the radial artery in his arm. He will be returning as soon as he has recovered enough to walk. They are giving him a blood transfusion."

Laughter still hovered in Kiroyo's eyes.

"So," Shenlyn said, "so it has come to this. My most brilliant surgeon and my oldest friend turn against me to defend a girl. Why? Kiroyo, why?"

Kiroyo had not time to answer him. There came a pounding on the door. Renson opened it and Cromer propelled Andra into the room with such force that she staggered and fell on the floor.

"Violence?" Shenlyn remarked calmly. "Surely there is no need for violence, Cromer?"

Cromer did not answer him immediately but slammed the door. Kiroyo noted the pallor of his face, the blue bruise under his eye, and the sweet-smelling surgical dressing on his arm. Cromer's thin lips were grim.

"Violence is needed to answer violence. They've had my blood, Shenlyn. Soon they'll be coming for yours."

"Who?"

"The young people."

Shenlyn shrugged.

"And you tremble at the knees because of a handful of young people?"

Cromer's steely eyes flashed.

"Don't underestimate them, Shenlyn. They're out of hand. Already they've overrun therapy.

They've smashed every computer in the place. Linli has a broken nose and three attendants are bleeding. They won't listen to Lascaux and they wouldn't listen to me. They howled at us to release the girl."

"And where might your security men be?"

"They're there. They're trying to restore order but I don't think they stand much chance. The young ones use violence. Two of my men were concussed as they entered the building, hit over the head with a drawer from the filing cabinet. Shenlyn, they are not just a handful of young people. There are hundreds. When they find the girl's gone they'll be coming here."

He pointed to the girl with dark hair who sat beside Kiroyo.

"She's the canker in their minds, the rot which drives them insane. Lascaux refused to rehabilitate her. I left through the back door and brought her here."

Shenlyn spared Andra one swift glance of distaste and went to the window. There was a click as the blinds flew upwards and he stood in brooding silence staring down at the grey emptiness of Administration Square. Cromer joined him. The other Administrative deputies talked in short disjointed sentences, now and then pausing to regard the strange girl who had come among them. She wore a dress which shimmered in the light and her arms and legs were bare. Renson smiled at her but she didn't smile back. He was Shenlyn's deputy and she despised him. She bent her head towards the old man.

"Are you glad I'm back, Papa Kiroyo?"

Cromer heard her words and his stomach churned at such sentimentality. He had found out about Andra. She was the product of an unauthorised love affair and Dr Lascaux's brain graft. She was a mistake that should not have happened and should be rectified or erased.

Shenlyn, too, heard her words and it galled him to think that he may have to depend upon what Kiroyo said she knew. So the young people would be coming here. He thought of the girl in the room behind him and knew what he would do. The solution was sublimely simple.

Renson began to rewind the spool of film. He guessed Shenlyn would swallow his pride and allow the girl to see it . . . the planet their ship had found. He guessed Shenlyn would have to swallow his pride if he wished the ships to leave within the next six months.

Cromer nodded to the street below.

"There they are. They haven't wasted much time. There's your handful of young people, Shenlyn. A mob!"

"So, let them come," Shenlyn replied.

Cromer scowled.

"It's not pleasant having your arm ripped open, Shenlyn."

"I don't intend to have my arm ripped open.

218

Kiroyo, bring the girl who delights your eyes and addles your mind. They can have her back."

Cromer spluttered but Shenlyn opened the door and threw Andra a mocking bow. With a haughty toss of her head she swept past him and led the way along the high light corridors of Administration. Shenlyn, Cromer and Kiroyo followed her.

There were about three hundred young people massed in Administration Square. Together they were like a restless creature which pawed the ground and turned hostile eyes on the largest building in the city: the place where Shenlyn was and the place where Cromer had taken Andra.

There was a low cheer as Andra appeared on the top of the steps and an angry mutter as Shenlyn and Cromer appeared behind her.

"Your friends seem pleased to see you," Shenlyn said. "Go and join them."

She stood and surveyed the mass of fair heads.

"And lose a perfect opportunity? If I ask them what they want they will answer me. Kids, what do you want?"

"Shenlyn out!"

In a body the young people moved nearer to the steps where Shenlyn was standing. The smile on Shenlyn's face was mocking them.

"Go down and bring the two leaders here to me," he told her.

The movement of the crowd ceased as she walked slowly down the flight of steps and walked back up again between Syrd and Daëmon. Shenlyn met them still sporting his amused smile.

"I believe you wish to air your grievances?"

"We have come to demand our rights as human beings," Daëmon said quietly.

His face was arrogant and his bearing was proud. Shenlyn was struck by the calm confidence of the boy who led the young people. His control over them was perfect. Daëmon was a born leader.

"Then demand. I am listening."

"We demand a complete revision of Administration which will give us the freedom of choice and the freedom of speech. We no longer wish to be just the mass-produced end products of EDCO."

Shenlyn nodded to the crowd.

"I assume you are united in your cause. Tell them to return to work and come inside with me."

Daëmon's chin tilted a little higher.

"So you refuse?"

Shenlyn smiled a slow smile.

"On the contrary. The things you demand you can have."

Andra stepped forward with narrowed eyes and there was a flush of anger on Cromer's face.

"Shenlyn, what game are you playing with us?" Andra asked.

"No game," Shenlyn replied. "I don't play games with children."

He turned on his heel and strode back into the building.

"So now what do we do?" Syrd asked.

"Go back to your work," Cromer growled.

Andra shook her head.

"Now we are here we can take Administration just as we took Therapy." She undid the brooch on her frock. "For your other arm, Cromer," she said, showing him the pin.

Kiroyo shook his head.

"Andra, violence belongs to the uncivilised times. It has no need to exist now. Do as Shenlyn asked. Tell the young ones to return to their work and come inside."

Syrd said:

"You expect us to listen to that lying . . ."

Kiroyo said quietly:

"I don't think Shenlyn would lie, Syrd. If he says you can have the things you demand then you can have them. He does not play games with children."

"But Shenlyn wouldn't give in to us just like that," Andra argued. "What does he mean?"

"That I can't tell you, but you might at least give him the chance to explain."

"You are asking us to come in and talk to Shenlyn, Papa Kiroyo?"

The old man nodded his head.

"Then we'll come. We'll come because you have asked us."

Daëmon turned to the crowd.

"Go back to your work. We are going to talk with Shenlyn. If we need you we will come."

Cromer watched as the young people slipped away between the ring of security men who surrounded the Square. From high above, in the room at the top of the building, Shenlyn also watched. They would have the things they demanded if the girl knew enough to enable them to survive.

26

"Sit down," Cromer instructed the three young people.

Syrd perched uneasily on the edge of a chair, eyes cast to the floor to avoid the stares of the officials of Sub-city One. Daëmon watched the Director pacing the floor, chin in hand, frowning at his thoughts at which Daëmon could not even guess. Andra walked in with Kiroyo, ignoring everyone, and seated herself beside the old man. Cromer wanted to shake her. Her impudence was infuriating. She would pass by the Director of Sub-city One as if she did not recognise him.

Shenlyn stood still.

"I think we will discuss your demands a little later. Now I have something to show you which no one outside this room has seen. Two of you will not recognise the things you see, they are beyond the conception of your imagination."

Renson switched off the lights and the room was submerged in total darkness. Cromer had never been in the dark before. His darkness had been the dim blue light from the ceilings above him. He had never seen the night in the overworld when the stars and the moon were veiled by clouds and human eyes were incapable of seeing even their own hands. His sense of helplessness was immense until on to the screen at the far end of the room came a flicker of light and he was able to distinguish vague shapes within the darkness.

Shenlyn spoke to the girl.

"Kiroyo informs me that you will recognise the things you are about to see. I have yet to be convinced, but if you do I wish you to tell us all you know. If you require the movement halted or the focus brought closer you will ask. You understand?"

She did not reply.

"Girl, do you understand?"

She said:

"I am not an idiot. I understand my native language when I hear it."

The light on the screen began to move. Syrd and Daëmon listened to Andra. Her low magic voice always painted pictures in their minds, but now the pictures were there before their eyes. They watched in fascination, spellbound by forms and colours they had never seen before. But it was Andra who made it real.

"A planet which draws nearer. A planet with two moons. I don't recognise the constellations. The planet is not Earth, the light is too bright and the continent masses are different."

The coloured orb became obscured by a cloud mass until the ship which had taken the film sank below it.

"That is a polar ice cap. The land is covered by

ice and snow many hundreds of feet thick. The temperatures are below freezing and the wind whips up the snow in clouds. Conditions are similar to those on Earth, it is cold beyond human endurance. We have passed over the ice desert to the cliffs by the sea and even the salt water is frozen over. Now it breaks into floes of ice and bergs. The open sea. There is an island of barren rock. Stop! Can you take it nearer?"

Her sharp eyes had spotted a movement and the island rushed towards them. Kiroyo knew what she would see but Cromer was still ignorant. This was the film produced from a tiny microfilm they had retrieved from the wrecked space ship. At the present moment he was seeing the planet 801 but he had no idea what he would see. A bird wheeled into the air and dived into the sea, startling him from his indifference.

"Kiroyo!" Andra's voice came as a gasp of excitement. "Kiroyo! Did you see that! A bird! A sea bird! And look! There are more birds on the cliff by the sea. A whole colony of them. It must be a nesting site."

Shenlyn watched her profile as the film sped across the sea. Kiroyo had said she would know and it seemed she did.

And on they went over the vast expanse of moving ocean, dark grey, green, sparkling blue, now caught by the sun in glittering swelling movement, now caught by the clouds to a dull ripple of grey rollers and by the wind to waves tipped with foam until they reached the land again. Shenlyn saw her lips moving in the darkness.

"Coniferous forests: pine, spruce and fir. I can't tell which at this height. Now the grasslands of the cold zone, wide prairies bounded by mountains on the right. Stop! Take it down! Look at that, Papa Kiroyo! Ruminants: a whole herd of them. I would call them bison but they have horns like the moose. Kiroyo, what is this place?"

Shenlyn gave him no time to reply.

"A ruminant? What's that?"

She said:

"A herbivore, that is, a grass-eater. They have many stomachs and regurgitate their food to chew cud. Man domesticated them for their meat and milk. They were also used as beasts of burden to plough the fields and carry. Their hides were used for making a weather-proof material called leather. These particular species I would say are too wild to tame."

Shenlyn didn't even know what fields were. She had to tell him. Then the film went on over ranges of fold mountains which were peaked with snow. She took them down to an inland lake which reflected trees and the sky. The climate here, she told them, was milder as some of the trees were deciduous and shed their leaves in the cold season. On over autumn forest they went, waving gold and yellow under the wind. Then the sun rippled with the wind over vast subtropical grasslands she called savannah. She pointed out a ring of primitive huts where she said people must live. Long-horned cattle roamed in their thousands. And on to tropical jungles and snaking rivers to catch a glimpse of an animal she called a cat and see trees laden down with fruit she stated were citrus: lemons, oranges and grapefruit. They saw plants she identified as sweet corn, sugar cane, tea, tobacco, rice and potatoes. She knew their food content and how they were cooked. To the sea they went where a host of small green islands floated on sandy beaches. Palm trees hung with nuts and fruit; birds flashed through the leaves; creatures crept, crawled or ran in a world of sunshine. She knew and named them all.

She knew the climatic conditions and the soil fertility. She knew the food value of wheat, beans and cabbage. She could recognise the edible fruits. She knew how to cook and make fire. She knew how to plant and harvest crops. Of geology she was a little more vague, but she would guess at the wealth of minerals which lay below the surface. They bombarded her with questions and she could answer them all. She was amazed at their ignorance and astounded them with her knowledge. She took them on a magic trip around a world they had not even dreamed of, and when the screen went blank their minds were bursting with the things they had learnt and stars of colour flickered before their eyes.

Renson switched on the lights and Cromer was

staring at her, awed by the things she knew. Kiroyo felt the pressure of her hand and was proud Andra had not failed. Syrd and Daëmon still stared at the screen like beings hypnotised. Shenlyn looked down on her, a mere girl child, whom he had despised not twenty minutes before.

"Well, lady, could we live there? Could we start a community which would support itself?"

There was wonder in her eyes and she did not seem to hear him. Kiroyo touched her arm.

"Tell him what he wants to know, Andra."

The officials of Sub-city One stared at the girl with dark eyes. They no longer felt repulsed by her appearance. Appearance didn't matter, only the things she knew.

"That place," Andra said to the blank screen, "is like the earth was after the last ice age. The people there are primitive. Compared with us they are ignorant but they have found a way to live."

"And could *we* live there?"

She turned towards him, the big man with frowning brows.

"That is a world of virgin soil and gentle weather. Of course we could live there. Any fool could see that."

Shenlyn raised a fist to Kiroyo.

"You knew! All the time you knew!"

"I did not. So perhaps I recognised the wheat plant and remembered how to make flour, but I certainly didn't remember how to make bread. I would have found out for you but I didn't know. And Andra speaks with a rash tongue. So maybe she is confident she could live there, but she forgets that the people of Sub-city One do not know how."

"They will find out," Andra said. "If they aren't taught then they experience trial and error. Some die, some live. Does it matter how many die as long as some live?"

"And you are as heartless as Shenlyn, Andra," Kiroyo told her.

Renson said:

"I assume we go ahead with our original plans, Shenlyn?"

"Of course." Shenlyn turned to Daëmon. "And there is freedom, Daëmon. There are the human rights you so forceably demand. The planet we call 801 is yours. There you will be able to live as you please far away from myself and Administration. In six months one thousand young people will leave this earth for that planet. It is far away in another galaxy. It will take them thirty years of travelling through space to get there, and you will be with them. Personally I think I am giving you a paradise. I even envy you and wish I was young enough to come."

Cromer poured himself a drink. He had listened in silence and inside he was seething. In six months the ships would leave earth.

"And you give that paradise to a bunch of

headstrong children, Shenlyn? Why are you suddenly so noble?"

Shenlyn scowled at the man in the rich purple uniform.

"Not so noble, Cromer. I use my common sense. I send the young ones. Young they will be when they leave, but when they reach 801 they will be adult men and women. Their children will be born on the journey and grow up in a world of sunlight. It is not these children here who will benefit, but their children after them. You would have me send the old ones who will maybe die before they arrive? Old men too feeble to build shelter or provide food? Old women incapable of giving birth? Oh no, Cromer, much as it grieves me, that place will not be for you and me."

Daëmon was stunned. Someone put a drink in his hand and it spilled on his tunic. There were people all around him, talking, laughing, and all he could see were the pictures which swirled through his mind. Shenlyn was giving them that place, the glory of colour and living things, thirty years across the void of space they would be going to live on another world beneath another star.

"A city of clear plastic," Syrd said. "By the sea or by a river. Daëmon, can't you see it?"

"And insects," Andra said, "which carry stings. Insects which bring disease. Snakes with a poisonous bite. Animals which hunt our flesh. Germs which fly on the teeth of the wind. It won't be so easy."

230

Daëmon regarded her dark laughing eyes.

"Are you afraid, Andra?"

"No," she said.

"And you'll have Linli," Shenlyn remarked.

"Linli has an awful lot to learn," she replied.

Shenlyn handed her a drink.

"And you will teach Linli? You will teach them all?"

"I'll teach them."

Shenlyn nodded. She would teach them and they would survive. He did not want any of them to die. He was not too proud to admire their confidence and their courage. Nor was he too proud to sincerely wish them luck.

"We'll drink," Shenlyn said as he raised his glass, "to the future: planet 801, the young people who go there and the ships that will take them. But most of all we will drink to you, Andra."

He smiled at the girl who had seen so much. They were not her eyes at all but the eyes of a boy who had died two thousand years ago and would live on for maybe another thousand more. Without Andra there was no future, for without her they could not survive on planet 801.

"And whilst you remain in Sub-city One," Shenlyn added, "you will obey my rules."

Andra turned to Kiroyo.

"Must I have my hair cut off, Papa Kiroyo?"

Kiroyo murmured:

"If you wish to keep it long then you keep it long. Your power is greater than Shenlyn's. You

231

are indispensable, my little Andra. Even I must bow before you."

The old man bowed his head and shuffled away. Andra followed him.

"Papa Kiroyo, where are you going?"

"Back to my books."

"I'll come with you."

He shook his head. His hair was no longer greying, it was white.

"You will be needed here, child. You will be needed for so many things. You must work with Shenlyn to prepare for a journey to a star. I will be needed with my books, for even you do not know everything. You will come before you go and say goodbye."

She watched him walk away along the straight white corridor, an old man with shambling steps and bowed head. There was a lump in her throat and she wanted to cry. When she went to 801 she must leave Papa Kiroyo behind. She turned back to the room and tried not to see the empty chair where he had been sitting.

Cromer honoured her with a mechanical smile. Andra was beyond his reach. She would be guarded as closely as Shenlyn himself. Andra he could not touch, but the boy Syrd was still vulnerable.

ANDRA

27

Cromer leaned back in the chair, his feet propped up on a stool before him. He had been glad of this day of relaxation to put the finishing touches to his weeks of careful planning. He had also been glad to escape to the comfort of his luxury apartment and be relieved from the duty of inspecting the twelve great silent ships on the cold bay below the surface. He had waited six months for this day to come. Today would see the culmination of his efforts and the destruction of a thousand dreams. Cromer smiled.

The man in the white tunic said:

"Your thoughts amuse you, Cromer?"

"A little. Go into the other room. He will be here any minute."

The medical orderly saluted and obeyed. His feet made no sound on the soft carpet. Still Cromer smiled to himself, although he was not pleasantly anticipating the coming invasion of his privacy. He looked upon it as an irritation which had to be borne but was a very necessary irritation.

He slowly revolved in the swivel chair and his apartment became a blur of brown and gold. He stopped to stare at the fish which swam within a wall of water and regarded him with quietly shining eyes. The weeds and the water rippled with their movements. He swung to the opposite wall where glass doors led to the balcony and garden. He could see hanging plants reflected in a turquoise pool. The light outside was dim and blue. Soon he would have to go, obliged by his position to make an appearance at the dance hall. That, too, was a distasteful necessity. Cromer disliked dancing. But first the interview. The boy was late.

He rang for a drink and his personal attendant came immediately to pour a yellow liquid into a delicate glass, bow and retire. Cromer sipped, it was sweet and palatable, and above its yellow surface he could study the landscape painting which glowed with quiet colours. He had kept it because it pleased his eye. The girl he detested but her painting he could lean back and admire.

"Come in!"

His personal attendant ushered the boy in.

"Sit down," Cromer instructed.

The boy sat on the brown divan. His eyes roamed restlessly round the room to watch the lazy fish blowing bubbles on the wall and recognise the painting as one which had hung in the youth centre: Andra's painting.

"What do you want?" Syrd asked.

He was not supposed to leave the computer room when he was on duty.

"You are on duty in the main computer room this evening?" Cromer asked.

"Yes. Until Hanman returns. Why?"

"Is there anyone else on duty with you?"

"Hanman. He was called away. He will be returning shortly."

"Ah yes! I asked him to check the computer in my office. It will take him at least an hour. So you are on your own?"

"Why?"

"I want those ships destroyed."

Cromer watched the disbelief in Syrd's eyes. It gave him a sense of power. The boy had not known he worked for Grovinski. He didn't know that was why Cromer had allowed him to live. Had he thought the head of security in Sub-city One was an idiot? Cromer knew why he had come here. Cromer knew everything about him there was to know. He should have wrecked that ship completely but one tiny microfilm had escaped. Enough to show them all they needed to know about planet 801. So far Syrd had not proved very efficient.

"Did you hear what I said?"

"I heard."

"I want those ships destroyed immediately."

Syrd stood up.

"I want nothing to do with it."

Cromer had been expecting such a reaction.

"Have you forgotten why you were sent here?"

"I try to."

Cromer polished his nails with a soft cloth. So the young Uralian had changed sides. Cromer knew why. That girl Dr Lascaux had created had even softened Shenlyn's austere nature. She must have found it very easy to steal Syrd's loyalty for herself. Cromer supposed he should try to reason with the boy. He sensed it would do no good and there were other ways. The prize which dangled before his eyes was too big to be ignored. Planet 801 had been claimed by Grovinski before Shenlyn even knew it existed. For the last ten years Uralia had been preparing for an exodus now only two years away. He, Cromer, would be the first Director of the city they would build there. He had been offered a world to control in return for his services, and a mere boy was not going to foil his ambition.

"You will destroy those ships," Cromer said quietly.

"You're mad," Syrd said. "In six weeks those ships are leaving for 801 and I'm going with them."

"You can still go to that planet on the Uralian ships."

"And be ruled by Grovinski's narrow-minded restrictions? Not likely! You forget, Cromer, I know what it's like to live under Uralian rule. It's as dismal as hell. No, thank you! Once, when I didn't know better, your bribe might have worked. But not now."

Cromer's expressionless eyes did not flicker.

238

"You will do as you are told."

"You don't scare me, Cromer. I'm not doing your dirty work. I'm leaving this room now and I'm going straight to Shenlyn."

"Sit down! The doors are sealed. You cannot leave."

Syrd clenched his fist.

"So Grovinski was mistaken to trust you," Cromer mused. "Your loyalty to Uralian supremacy has seeped away. How foolish. 801 belongs to Grovinski."

"801 belongs to no one," Syrd said. "It's free and I'm going there. We're all going there. I'm not blasting those ships and destroying everything we've worked for."

"You will not be going anywhere," Cromer said. "Nor will that black-eyed female who has so enchanted your eyes you can no longer see reason."

"Leave Andra out of this. She's got nothing to do with it. I won't sabotage those ships, Cromer."

"I am sorry," Cromer said, "but you have no choice."

He snapped his fingers.

"What do you mean I have no choice? I can choose between what's right and what's wrong. I won't . . ."

Syrd ended with a gasp. He had not seen the man or heard him. He hadn't known he was there until the needle pierced the thin tunic and stabbed into his arm. He turned with a vicious sweep of his fist, but the person was blurred and indistinct, too far for him to reach. There was a rushing in his head and he sat down heavily.

"That was the tranquillising injection?" Cromer asked.

The man nodded.

Syrd heard and saw them from miles away. The room was turning dark. He did not see the man kneel before him but he could distinguish the light which swam before his eyes. The man swung the light slowly to and fro. Syrd watched it, dazed with the desire to sleep but fighting it with a greater desire to watch that floating swinging light. It was brilliant yellow. It went from left to right, from right to left, slowly, slowly, to and fro. The light, the swinging light, warm and yellow, nothing more. Slower, slower, slower, until it stopped. Syrd was calm and utterly empty.

Cromer listened to the silence then leaned across the table.

"Syrd, can you hear me?"

"Yes. I can hear you."

"You are familiar with the workings of the computer which has been built to control the twelve space ships which will shortly leave for the planet 801, are you not?"

"Yes. I am qualified in computer electronics."

"You would know how to set the computer for a routine launch?"

"Yes. I am qualified in computer electronics."

"You will go now to the computer room and

set the computer to fire the motors of the twelve ships at 2200 hours. The ships will commence a routine launch at 2200 hours. What will you do?"

"I will go to the computer room and set number six computer to launch its ships at 2200 hours."

"You are confident you can do that?"

"Yes. I am qualified in computer electronics."

Cromer consulted a paper on his desk.

"The computer which controls the roof of the launching bay is also in the same room, is it not?"

"Yes. Number twenty-three computer controls the roof of the main cavern."

"You will set that computer to open the roof four minutes before the ships lift off. What will you do?"

"I will set number six computer to launch its ships at 2200 hours. I will set number twenty-three computer to open the roof at 2156."

"Good. I perceive you understand my instructions. Talk to no one on your way there. After you have done what I ask, you will go to the youth centre and dance. At 2200 hours you will return to your apartment and sleep. When you wake you will remember nothing of this evening. Now go!"

28

It was late in the evening. Outside in the streets
the light had been dim blue for over an hour, but
on the top floor of Administration it still glowed
white. Andra rested her elbows on the desk and
her chin in her hands and let the ghastly tiredness
seep through her. The room was quiet except for
the rustle of the closely printed paper Linli was
studying. She had not noticed when the people in
pale blue uniforms went away. The room without
people was enormous, but to Andra it was still a
close confine of ceiling and walls.

She wanted to get out. Why did she want to get
out? It was just a vague unease that had settled
over her, urging her to go. She forced the craving
from her mind and concentrated on the symptoms
of yellow fever, snake-bite, typhoid fever, malaria
and cholera. There were only six weeks left and
Linli had masses to learn. Just six short weeks and
then thirty long years before they reached the sun.
The passage of time stretched ahead like eternity.

The last few months she had driven them relent-
lessly. Crammed their minds with the things they
had to know. She had raged and shouted when
they didn't understand. Not many hours ago she
had called Daëmon an ignorant lout and he would

no longer speak to her. She had driven them just as the thoughts in her head drove her. Were they her thoughts? Or were they the thoughts of Richard Carson which Dr Lascaux had put there? For almost two years she had suffered a sense of loss and grief for the things that had gone and would not return. She had longed to get out, go up into the wind and breathe the air. But even greater than her longing had been the knowledge that the way of life in Sub-city One was all wrong. So she had been forced to start a rebellion and demand for herself the human rights restrictions had denied. And all the things she had asked for Shenlyn had given her, far away on another world revolving around another star.

Now she was feeling empty as if something had gone from her. It made her uneasy. It made her sense something was wrong, something was hanging over her, something awful, horrible and unavoidable. She felt sick with apprehension and she was so terribly tired.

She left the desk to pace the room, feeling suffocated by the warmth and the longing to go out.

"Why don't you rest?" Linli said.

His voice came drifting on the shadows of sleep. She didn't answer him but paced again to try to drive away the lassitude of her mind. Her silver tunic reflected the light and she gazed at the floor she did not see. She could no longer think or reason. Something was wrong.

The door at the far end flew open. Dr Lascaux was breathless.

"Is something wrong, Andra?"

She was startled. She hadn't heard him come in. She shook her head. Something was wrong but she didn't know what.

"I think," said Linli, "she's had enough. I told her to go home."

"It was just a hunch I had," Lascaux said. "Something told me I was needed here. Andra, sit down."

She obeyed him. The hunch was just an inexplicable sensing that screamed in her head like thundering doom and told her she had to go up. She had to go up and she didn't know why. Her hair was wet with sweat and her skin, when Lascaux touched her wrist, was icy cold. Her forehead was burning.

"Andra, when did you last eat?"

"An hour ago," Linli told him. "They brought us supper just after Shenlyn left."

"And sleep?"

"Days, weeks," Andra said. "I don't remember."

"Does your head ache?"

"Yes. No. I don't know. No, my head doesn't ache. It's empty."

"Empty?"

"Drained, empty. Richard Carson has gone. Something's going to happen. I must get out. It's hot in here."

She was staring at the ceiling. Linli too stared up. What was Andra babbling about? Lascaux pulled her to her feet.

"Come back with me to therapy. I'll give you an injection to make you sleep. You are working yourself into a state of collapse."

"And everyone else," muttered Linli. "She's a ruthless bully, Lascaux. You should try working with her. Even Shenlyn finds it difficult to keep up the pace. Yes, she's a bully."

"And she is also a human girl with human limitations. Andra, come on. They can manage here without you for twenty-four hours."

She walked in silence beside Dr Lascaux along the high light corridors of Administration, down countless stairs and down the steps outside into the comparative cool of the city. Kiroyo was crossing the Square on the way to his apartment. From the youth centre came the sound of music. The coolness seemed to revive her. She ought to find Daëmon, they had quarrelled and she couldn't remember why. And Kiroyo was here leaning on his stick and smiling at her. She thought how old and frail he looked.

"You look pale and tired, Andra. You are not ill, are you?"

His dark eyes questioned Lascaux.

"She is exhausted but I think she will survive."

Andra took the old man's hand.

"I haven't been to see you. I've been so busy. I haven't been to say goodbye, Papa Kiroyo."

He squeezed her slim white fingers.

"But you've six more weeks to say goodbye, Andra. Before you go you will come and have supper with Papa Kiroyo in his apartment, yes? Bring Syrd and Daëmon. I would like to talk to them again. I am losing touch with all my young friends."

Syrd crossed to the street which led to the youth centre. Andra watched him but did not call to him. Restlessly she pulled her hand away.

"That will be nice," she told Kiroyo. "But I must go now."

She slipped away before Lascaux could stop her, running up the dim blue streets. The surgeon bent and picked up the silver cloak which had fallen from her shoulders.

"Where does she go?" Kiroyo asked him. "Where does she run to through the night streets? Her apartment is the other way."

"I don't know," Lascaux said as she vanished into the blurred distance. "She says the boy I put in her head has gone. She goes chasing after a spirit, Kiroyo. She should come to therapy."

"Why did she say 'Goodbye'?" Kiroyo asked. "It worries me."

29

Daëmon, from the platform, surveyed the young people in the room below him. A few were dancing to the music from the machine. Others worked quietly at the tables or read translations of the books from the archives. This was a time of anti-climax, a time of waiting for the end and the beginning. Looking back the months had passed quickly, but the few weeks ahead seemed like a lifetime, an age of waiting for their journey to begin. Their conversation came to Daëmon in disjointed phrases merging with the rhythm of the music into a meaningless hum of sound.

Where was Andra? She had said she would come, and now the evening was almost over. Surely she wasn't still working in Administration? He fastened his cloak round him. The words that had passed between them rankled unpleasantly in his mind. He would go and look for Andra. It was time they were friends again. He left the lighted room and went into the dim blue streets. Syrd was coming towards him. Without a word of greeting Syrd went to open the door.

"Have you seen Andra?" Daëmon asked him.

Syrd paused with his hand outstretched and stared at Daëmon with no flicker of recognition in his eyes.

"Have you seen Andra?" Daëmon repeated.

"I am going to the youth centre," Syrd said in a dull flat voice. "I am going to the youth centre to dance."

Daëmon regarded him. Something was wrong: his voice, his whole appearance was wrong. His eyes were glassy and he seemed to be moving in a dream. It was as though Syrd could neither see him nor hear him and the only thought in his head was to go to the youth centre and dance. Daëmon moved in front of him to prevent him entering the room.

Syrd scowled at him.

"Let me through. I must go in and dance."

Daëmon waved his hand in front of Syrd's face. The blue eyes never blinked. He was in some kind of trance. Hypnotised maybe. And where was Andra? Daëmon felt a twinge of apprehension. He snapped his fingers impatiently and Syrd seemed startled. The vacant stare was gone.

"Hello, Daëmon."

"Well, put the flags out! So you do recognise me! I have been speaking to you for the last five minutes and all I had was a lot of rot about dancing. What's the matter with you?"

"Nothing."

"Then be good enough to answer my question."

"What question?"

Daëmon sighed.

"Have you seen Andra?"

"No. I don't think so. Yes, I have. Back in the Square. I can't remember."

"Surely you know what you saw with your own eyes?"

"I don't remember. My head aches. Yes, she was in the Square."

"You're quite sure?" Daëmon asked sarcastically. "How long ago?"

"This morning, yesterday, I'm not sure. Just now. I don't know but I saw her."

Daëmon stamped his foot.

"What's wrong with you? Why did Cromer want you? Where in the glory have you been all this time? I thought you were coming straight here."

"Cromer?" muttered Syrd. "I haven't seen Cromer."

"Of course you have. I was waiting for you to come off duty when the security man gave you the message. You went to his apartment over an hour and a half ago."

"But I haven't seen Cromer," Syrd said puzzled. "Why on earth would Cromer want to see me?"

"You tell me," Daëmon snapped. "You're idiotic!"

"I'm not," Syrd protested. "I just can't remember a damned thing. Someone snapped their fingers. Was it you?"

"Oh, go to bed!" Daëmon growled. "I'm going to find Andra."

He strode away towards the open precinct of Administration Square. Syrd stared after him. If he was looking for Andra he was going the wrong way. Andra would be in their apartment by now. The clock on the wall said 2143. Where had he been for more than an hour and a half? He could remember Hanman being called away and himself offering to stay on, but after that he could recall nothing and his head ached with trying to remember.

In the Square Daëmon hesitated. His eyes roamed over the gleaming façade of the Administration building, up across the countless windows blazing with light, up to the quiet blue above him and the roof he could not see. The light was as blue as the dress she had been wearing the day of their revolution, it moved through a million shades from dark to pale. Her voice had come through a swirl of black hair: "You don't understand, for a moment it was all green, warm, heavy, singing green, everywhere mixed with the sun. If I could only have reached him I need never have come back." Where was Andra? Why did he remember those strange words she had said, words he had never understood? They had made him feel afraid then and they made him feel afraid now.

"You look for stars, eh, Daëmon?"

Daëmon was startled to see Kiroyo beside him and Dr Lascaux with a silver cloak draped over his arm. It was like being wakened in the middle of a dream.

Syrd took his arm.

"I've just remembered official working time ends at 2000 hours."

"I know that."

"Andra will be in our apartment."

"Are you looking for Andra?" Kiroyo asked. "A moment ago she was here with us. Dr Lascaux was taking her to therapy, she has been working too hard. But it seems she did not want to go to therapy and she did not want to stay and talk to a stuffy old man. She rushed away. She did not say where she was running to but it was not to your apartment. She went quite the other way."

"Huh!" said Syrd. "So we have the whole of the Sub-city in which to seek her. We seek her here, we seek her there. We seek her all night. I'm not playing peek-a-boo with Andra. I'm going to bed."

"Andra and I had a quarrel," Daëmon said. "I wished to find her."

"And you look for her in the sky?" Lascaux asked.

"I just looked up," Daëmon said.

"Because you sense she is there?"

"She looks for a spirit," Kiroyo murmured. "And where else would a spirit be but in the sky?"

"Oh, blow Andra!" Syrd said. "She'll come back sometime."

"But where is she?" Daëmon asked.

251

"I think she has gone up," Lascaux said.

"Up?" Daëmon repeated. "Up to the cavern? The rocket site?"

"Maybe. And maybe not. I expect she will be back."

Syrd was alarmed. He looked around him wildly.

"Now what's wrong?" Daëmon asked him.

"I don't know. I only know she mustn't go to the rocket site. I don't know why. I've got to stop her."

"For Pete's sake explain," Daëmon demanded.

Syrd started running.

"Where are you going?" Daëmon called.

"Andra! Come and help me. She mustn't go there."

He disappeared into the blue distance. With an apologetic glance Daëmon followed him. Lascaux listened to their feet pounding away along the metal road and waited for the silence to surge back. He took Kiroyo's arm and together they took the curving road away from the Administration building in slow pursuit.

"We'll go and find her," Lascaux said. "It will put your mind at rest, my friend. You can ask her why she said goodbye."

30

Andra ran along the road which curved upwards past the luxury apartments of the upper social circle. After she was half way, she remembered it was not the quickest way to the stairs, but now it would be no quicker if she turned back. A dance hall gave out its happy inhabitants who laughed in the forecourt. The doors stood open and inside the musicians were still playing Boria's electronic symphony. She hardly saw the brilliant flashes of colour within the light. The head of security was dancing inside as Andra elbowed her way through the crowd. Shenlyn, standing by his car, saw her and called her name. She had no time. She had to go up. She squeezed between two women in purple tunics and ran on along the almost empty road.

Renson said:

"Our lady Andra is not in a sociable mood tonight."

"And she should not be out in the streets at this hour," Shenlyn snapped. "Where does she think she's going without a bodyguard?"

"Therapy, perhaps? Or to see her friend in the design department? Kiroyo's rooms?"

"Not Kiroyo's. She's passed by them. The

design department will bc closed at this time of night and why should she go to therapy?"

"Well, the factories then? Perhaps she has taken it into her head to inspect the hatchets or the ploughshares."

Shenlyn started the motor.

"Get in, Renson."

"My apartment isn't far. I can easily walk."

"Get in. Something is going on. My right palm is itching."

Renson laughed.

"So scratch it," he said.

Shenlyn was not to be humoured.

"That girl," he said, "is up to something. Something is going on that shouldn't bc. She's going to the ships, Renson."

"How do you know?"

"I have a hunch."

"But why should she?"

"I can't imagine."

"But she can't go there, Shenlyn. The daylight is switched off. She'll freeze. She wasn't even wearing a cloak. I think your hunch is a little wrong."

"Get in, Renson," Shenlyn repeated. "Dr Lascaux is always saying: if you have a hunch, stick to it. I say she is going to the ships."

Renson was staring along the road.

"You talk of the devil and the devil comes: Lascaux himself."

"Where?"

"There! On the other side of the forecourt with Kiroyo."

Lascaux raised a hand in recognition and guided the old man through the crowd towards the car.

"Have you seen Andra? I believe she must have come this way. I was taking her with me to therapy and she suddenly ran off."

Renson said:

"The lady Andra passed us a few minutes ago, head bent to the ground and footsteps running. She had a quarrel with Daëmon today so she scowls at the ground and speaks to no one. Our Director is annoyed. She had no security guards with her."

"I sent them away," Lascaux remarked. "I told you, she was to come with me to therapy."

"So you have seen the hare," Kiroyo murmured. "Have you also seen the hounds who follow the hare?"

"What?" said Shenlyn.

"Daëmon and Syrd who run after Andra? She goes to the rocket site and they try to stop her. Maybe they have gone the other way. It is quicker."

"So you see, Renson," Shenlyn said triumphantly, "it seems my hunch was right. She is going to the rocket site."

"We are not sure," Lascaux said. "She was in a strange mood. She is making herself ill with overwork."

"Then wherever she is going," Shenlyn said,

"she has no right to be going there. You wish her to go to therapy, Lascaux, then to therapy she will go. We will go and find our Andra."

Renson, Lascaux and Kiroyo climbed into the car. Shenlyn reversed and free-wheeled down the slope back into the great Square.

"I think this way is quickest."

Andra had run through the back streets behind the factories and up the steep slopes behind the mechanical workshops. The city was still and quiet, and her pounding feet echoed loudly on the metal roads. She was gasping for breath by the time she reached the escalator. She paused a moment and wondered why on earth she had come haring through the outskirts of the Sub-city and left Daëmon waiting for her at the youth centre. She was being stupid, but she looked up the escalator and knew she had to go on up.

She clung to the moving handrail and heard voices and footsteps faint from the distance but coming nearer. The stairs took her up and the voices faded away. The dim blue light behind her was empty. Why was she going up? Even now her common sense told her to return the way she had come, but the unease which lay heavily in her stomach wouldn't let her. There was something wrong. Up there! She had to go up.

"Andra!" Daëmon called.

She turned and saw him far below. She started to run, doubling the speed of the stairs still too high for her to see their end. Again she glanced back. There were two people but they had come no nearer. She doubted if they could even see her.

"Andra!" Syrd's voice came to her like the whisper of the night wind in the overworld. "Andra, for pity's sake come back. Don't go in there! Andra! Don't go in there!"

Her heart was thumping loudly against her ribs and her legs ached from climbing. She could see the top now. She remembered the last time she had come here with Papa Kiroyo to see the sun. Dr Lascaux had told her Richard Carson didn't exist, but even from the time when her eyes had been bandaged she had sensed he was there and then she had actually seen him. He had been standing on the bridge across the stream which had led to his grandfather's house. He had been watching the water and waiting for her. And the world was just like it *had* been, there was grass, and trees singing with birds, and green sunlight everywhere. She had almost reached him but Shenlyn had pulled her back and everything had gone. There was only the snow and the cold cruel emptiness. And whose thoughts now drove her upwards? Her own? Or the boy who had lived far back along the passages of time? Was it he or she who sensed something was wrong? Where was he?

She stumbled on to the landing, pressed the button to open the door and passed from the warm city into the immense cold cavern. Her eyes swept round its dimness to pick out the forms of the twelve spaceships. They were dark in the darkness, towering slim and smooth towards the roof. Their massive bulks were almost hidden in wreaths of smoke which curled and drifted nearer to her and increased in density with every passing second.

From the stairs Syrd was calling to her, but she did not move. She just stood and stared, numb with horror.

The ships were leaving. They were leaving and she couldn't go with them. They were going to that beautiful planet and she would be left behind. Everyone would be left behind. Twelve empty hulls would sail away through space and leave a thousand young people behind with just their dreams. With a lump in her throat she looked upwards to see the sky and the stars. There was no sky and no stars. She could only see the roof. The ships couldn't leave. There was no way out for them. Above them was five hundred feet of rocks and concrete. They couldn't reach the stars; only explode: explode with a force of fire which would destroy half the city beneath them.

She swung with all her strength on the lever which opened the roof. The smoke reached her, burning hot, pouring down her throat and making her choke. Through the open door she saw Syrd and Daëmon reach the landing. They were calling to her but she couldn't hear them. With desperation she strained downwards. It was 2156 hours. The roof opened slowly, letting in a rush of biting cold. The door back to the city automatically closed. Syrd and Daëmon were gone and there was no way out for her.

She retched, and staggered through the swirling heat and cold. There was no way back, her only hope was the tunnel which would lead her to the open spaces above and the icy frozen world. She ran through the fumes and smoke towards the unlit road. She stumbled over loose stones and felt the cold numbing her face and freezing her hands. The poisoned air stung her eyes and made her senses reel. She knew no distance and no time, only the compulsion which drove her on.

She struck at the button and clawed at the door which opened before her.

There was a ghost of a moon riding silver and high. Low on the horizon were the last traces of a sunset and trees etched against the pale sky, slightly swaying, smelling of resin and flowers. She heard a whippoorwill calling and river water rushing through its reeds. The air was vibrating like the strings of a guitar and a thousand living sounds made the music. From the shadow beneath the trees a horse nickered, and someone was coming towards her. He was a boy, almost a man, tall and dark. She knew who he was and she was glad she had come.

The wind screamed as Andra took three steps forward into the night and the swirling snow. The ground shook as she fell and her ears pounded with the noise. Twelve spaceships lifted slowly from the pit in the earth and reared into the sky with a flash of fire. She saw them as her tears turned to ice and the breath froze in her lungs. Her head fell forward and the black tumble of her hair was covered by the snow.

31

Shenlyn stopped the car at the foot of the escalator. The doors slammed. Renson peered up the stairs.

"There's no one up there."

"Remember the limits of your eyes," Lascaux reminded him.

"She's not here, nor are the boys. It was a ridiculous idea. Your hunch is wrong, Shenlyn."

"And where else can the girl be?"

"Anywhere within the twenty-mile circumference of the city."

Shenlyn glared at Renson. He nodded at the escalator.

"She is up there," Shenlyn said.

The Director opened the store cupboard beside the lift. He threw a heavy cape and a pair of gauntlets at his deputy and selected some for himself.

"You're not going up, Shenlyn?"

"I am. So are you."

"What? Up to the cavern at this time of night? It will be freezing up there. If we wait they will come down."

Shenlyn fastened the cloak around him.

"But the cold, Shenlyn. Even these will hardly

protect us. At least switch on the daylight and warm the place up a bit."

Renson flicked the switch and pulled on his massive gloves.

"It comes to something," Renson grumbled, "when the Director of a Sub-city has nothing better to do than play chasing games with a bunch of children."

Kiroyo wound down the window of the car.

"You are going up?" he inquired.

"Yes," said Shenlyn shortly. "You and Lascaux stay here."

They had almost reached the top when they heard the muffled roar. Shenlyn, with his hand on the rail, felt the vibrations of the noise.

"What's that?"

The roar rose to a screaming whine muted by the thick walls in between, then faded away. The Director was uneasy. He began to run up the stairs. The sound was like a rocket lifting off. What the hell was going on?

Syrd was pounding the door at the top. His fist made a muffled thudding. Already he knew it was useless. That noise, that awful screaming noise that went through and through him, making him shudder, told him it was useless. Andra was in there and the ships were taking off.

"Open! For pity's sake open, you bloody fool."

Daëmon threw his weight against it. It trembled slightly but would not open. Again and again he pressed the bright green button. Syrd's mood had filled him with a sense of urgency. The door wouldn't open but he had to open it and let Andra in.

Syrd rested his head against it.

"It's no good. Daëmon, it's no good. Andra . . ."

His voice trailed away.

Shenlyn strode up to them.

"What the devil are you doing here? Where's that confounded girl?"

Syrd looked up. His face was drawn and white.

"Andra is in there," he said. "And we can't open the damned door."

"Of course you can't," Renson remarked. "The roof must be open. The lever is down. This door can't be opened whilst the roof is open."

"The roof is open?" Shenlyn repeated. "Who opened the roof? Who opened the roof? And what was that noise?"

Renson pulled the lever. Faintly, far above them, they heard a thud.

"What was that noise?" Shenlyn demanded as he pressed the button.

"The ships," Daëmon whispered. "It must have been the ships. What else could it be?"

With a hiss the door before them opened. With terrible force the wind hit them, howling, screaming, shrieking, bitter with coldness and trying to drag their cloaks from their backs.

"The outer door must be open too," shouted Shenlyn.

Syrd started to run. Run. It was impossible, it was just a slow walk. It was an effort to move even one leg in front of the other against the wind. The breadth of the cavern seemed endless, a struggle of force against force, strength against strength. He was blinded by the wind. He groped along the wall to find the tunnel. And in the tunnel the wind was even stronger, a monster howling towards him and forcing him back. How far was it to the door? Andra was out there. He had to bring Andra in and close the door. His frozen hands clawed to find some finger-hold and the sweat on his face turned to ice. He was too cold even to think. Then the snow hit him, whirling whitely and viciously from the black circle of sky, blinding him, slashing his face, numbing his body, making him sink to his knees and give in.

Shenlyn saw him fall. He had shielded his eyes with his gloved hands and the great cloak was keeping away the bitterness of the cold. What fool had opened that door? Andra? Where was she? Where was that stupid girl?

The cold bit through his teeth as he pulled Syrd in from the snow. He felt his own body becoming numb and it took all his strength to force himself to take even two steps forward into the jaws of the blizzard. Was she here? Was Andra out here in this freezing cold? Again he shielded his eyes and raked the ground. He saw her shape almost completely covered with snow.

He took another step. The wind screamed around him and snatched the air away before he could breathe it. He bent, grasped her leg, and pulled her backwards and inside. He staggered to the wall and depressed the button. The outer door sighed shut and the night was gone. For a moment the relief to be free from the wind brought the blood rushing to his head and made him feel sick. He leant against the rock wall to recover.

"Are you all right?" Daëmon asked him.

He was coming down the tunnel, a black silhouette against the brightly lit cavern beyond.

"Yes," Shenlyn said. "Help your friend. He was a fool to come here with no cloak."

Daëmon helped Syrd to his feet and Shenlyn picked up Andra. Snow fell from her tunic and her hair as they went back along the rough road to the white light and the meagre warmth it gave. When he got her back to the city he would give her the hiding of her life. Her hair swayed as he walked and her limbs hung limp. The cold must have rendered her unconscious. No wonder! She was only wearing a tunic. She needed a thorough spanking.

"You found her then?" Renson said.

Shenlyn nodded and stepped on to the stairs. Behind him the door shut. He looked over his shoulder to Syrd and Daëmon coming behind.

"You will live?" he inquired of Syrd.

"Yes. And Andra?"

Shenlyn glanced down at her pale pointed face and closed eyes with their black lashes. She was a very important girl. She would have to live.

"The ships have gone, Shenlyn," Renson said. "All of them."

Shenlyn almost dropped her, so great was the shock.

"That was the noise we heard," Renson said. "All twelve of them taking off. She must have opened the roof and let them go."

The stairs took Shenlyn down and he wanted to hurl Andra to the bottom, destroy her as she had destroyed a lifetime of work and the hope of a whole city.

"Why?" Shenlyn asked. "Why? I offered her a world, everything she wanted, and in return she blasts twelve empty ships into space."

"No," Syrd said. "It wasn't Andra. It couldn't have been. Those ships can only be launched by remote control, from the computer room. Someone there must have set them off. Andra wouldn't know how to set a computer for a launching routine."

"He's right," said Renson. "The girl's not responsible. We ought to be thankful she went there. If she hadn't opened the roof they would have exploded. One hundred thousand tons of fuel would have exploded."

Syrd came down a few steps to join the Director.

"The roof can be opened by computer also," Syrd said dully. "There was no need for Andra to go in there." He touched her face. "She's frozen," he said, "and there was no need for her to go there at all."

Kiroyo saw them coming, moving shapes within the light which became Syrd, Daëmon and Renson, with Shenlyn carrying Andra. Lascaux opened the car door and Shenlyn handed her in. The black drift of her hair touched Kiroyo's face with a smother of coldness. Lascaux held her, the person he had created with a brain graft nearly two years ago. Andra, who could have died but had lived. He stared at her as Shenlyn took the driving seat beside Renson, and Syrd and Daëmon slipped into the long back bench. Why had Andra said goodbye to Kiroyo?

There was a moment of silence.

"Someone fired the ships," Shenlyn said. "Every bloody one of them."

They did not say anything. What was there to say? No amount of words could take away the stunned emptiness they felt. The leaving of the ships was the end of Kiroyo's three hundred years of work among the books, the end of Shenlyn's desire to create a new and better place, and for Syrd, Daëmon and Andra it was the end of the future and of planet 801. Lascaux felt Andra's pulse. When she realised what had happened how would she feel, this girl who had loved Kiroyo like a grandfather and changed a city full of robots back into human beings again?

Shenlyn remembered she was there.

"I'll drive you straight to therapy, Lascaux. It looks as though you'll be having Andra there for treatment after all."

Lascaux looked up, round at the ring of silent faces to meet the eyes of Shenlyn.

"Andra is dead," Lascaux said.

And the loss of planet 801 became just a little grief.

Also in
Lions Tracks

To order direct from the publisher, just tick the titles you want and fill in the order form on the last page.

LIONS · TRACKS

It's My Life

Robert Leeson

"You're playing hard to get," Sharon had said as Jan walked off, away from school and from Peter Carey's invitation to the college disco on Friday night. Was she? Jan didn't really know. She wanted time to think things out, ask Mum what she thought.

But when Mum doesn't come home, Jan finds her own problems taking second place, as she is expected to cope with running the house for her father and younger brother Kevin, as well as studying for exams and trying to sort out her feelings towards Peter. Slowly she realises what sort of life her mother led, the loneliness and the pressures she faced, and with this realisation comes Jan's firm resolve that despite the expectations of family, neighbours and friends, she will decide things for herself; after all, "It's my life."

An Inch of Candle

Alison Leonard

"We are now in the trenches again, and though I feel very sleepy I have just the chance to answer your letter, so I will while I may. It's really my being able to bag an inch of candle that incites me . . . I must measure my letter by the light."
Isaac Rosenburg, 28 March 1918

It is 1916 and young men everywhere are enlisting in the army and heading for the Front. Dora thinks it all so exciting and romantic and especially loves to read the letters from Humphrey, a gallant officer fighting in the trenches. That's why she finds it difficult to understand her "cowardly" brother, Richard, who refuses to fight. But all too soon Dora's views are challenged and for the first time she is forced to re-examine her principles.

All these books are available at your local bookshop or newsagent, or can be ordered from the publishers.

To order direct from the publishers just tick the titles you want and fill in the form below:

Name _____

Address _____

_____

Send to: Collins Children's Cash Sales
            PO Box 11
            Falmouth
            Cornwall
            TR10 9EN

Please enclose a cheque or postal order or debit my Visa/ Access –

  Credit card no:

  Expiry date:

  Signature:

– to the value of the cover price plus:

UK: 80p for the first book, and 20p per copy for each additional book ordered to a maximum charge of £2.00.

BFPO: 80p for the first book and 20p per copy for each additional book.

Overseas and Eire: £1.50 for the first book, £1.00 for the second book, thereafter 30p per book.

Lions Tracks